ECO-WORRIERS

Penguin Problems

Kathryn Lamb lives in Dorset with her children. As well as writing books, she draws cartoons for *Private Eye*, *The Oldie*, *The Spectator* and *The Blackmore Vale Magazine*.

Also available by Kathryn Lamb:

Best Mates Forever:
Love, Mates and Money
Vices and Virtues
Brothers, Boyfriends and Babe Magnets

Is Anyone's Family As Mad As Mine?

ECO-WORRIERS

Penguin Problems

Kathryn Lamb

Piccadilly Press • London

First published in Great Britain in 2007
by Piccadilly Press Ltd,
5 Castle Road, London NW1 8PR
www.piccadillypress.co.uk

A catalogue record for this book is available from the British Library

ISBN: 978 1 85340 918 9 (trade paperback)

3 5 7 9 10 8 6 4 2

Printed in the UK by CPI Bookmarque, Croydon, CR0 4TD

Cover design by Simon Davis
Typeset by M Rules, London

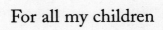
For all my children

Chapter One

It *was because* of the penguin.

Let me go back to the beginning. Not the beginning of time. That's too far. But I can go back as far as a few weeks . . .

I am lying on Evie's bed looking up at the penguin wallchart on her ceiling – there is no more room on the walls, every centimetre of which is covered by posters, wallcharts, shelves and cupboards full of books, cuddly toys and penguin paraphernalia. I am struggling to do up my jeans – I blame Mum for feeding me processed food (OK, so I nagged her into getting that pizza) but I hope she realises that Evie and I are serious about going organic – and I am serious about getting into shape for the Olympics. I want to win gold medals in swimming and athletics.

Evie is singing along to the latest track by our favourite singer, Dodo, who belts out powerful songs about changing the world and her own life.

'You stole my soul but I'm gonna get it back!' Evie yells, as the song comes to a punchy end. She loves Dodo's singing, and has posters of her on the walls along with the penguins – and a collection of all her CDs.

There is silence. A fly buzzes. It is stiflingly hot. Evie's curtains hang limply at the wide-open window.

'Smoothie?' Evie asks, opening her Koolsounds mini-fridge/CD player, and getting out two cartons of our favourite strawberry-and-mango smoothie.

'I thought you were going to ditch that fridge because it's non-eco-friendly,' I gasp, gratefully accepting the smoothie as I am exhausted and breathless from doing up my jeans. 'And because you're saving up for an MP3 player and speakers!'

'Yes – but if I get rid of it, where am I going to keep our smoothies? If I keep them in the fridge downstairs, Liam drinks them all. And I'll need another CD player so that I can listen to Dodo.'

Evie is sitting at her computer with her back to me, playing an online game called Ice-cream Pig, where you have to stop a cute little pig from getting hit on the head by a falling ice-cream scoop while you move him around the screen trying to catch the scoops in a cone.

'You certainly use up a lot of electricity!' I exclaim. 'You're *always* at the computer these days.' Evie's dad gave her his old prehistoric computer when he got an up-to-date, shiny new one – now he and Evie's brother Liam both have laptops.

'OK. Now you've made me feel guilty,' Evie grumbles. 'So I'm going to have to stick a black footprint on the chart, and I didn't want to.'

Evie has a wallchart and pull-out Eco-Guide from *Green Teen* magazine where you get to stick a green star on the wallchart if you or your family do something good for the environment – or a black footprint if you do something bad.

Eco-fact Number Three

The black footprint is a reference to the 'carbon footprint' which each household produces when they use electricity, gas and petrol made from non-renewable fossil fuels – coal and oil – the burning of which cause carbon emissions, which are trapped in the atmosphere and result in the 'greenhouse effect', otherwise known as global warming.

I didn't mean to upset Evie – global warming is obviously getting to me today. Feeling even hotter I go to stand beside the open window. This is not as easy as it sounds, as I have to clamber over a mound of assorted penguin and dolphin toys. Evie's last obsession was with dolphins – but she has now moved on to penguins. Most of the toys, books, posters, penguin stationery, etc. come from the Ecological Gardens, which is a local wildlife park for plants, birds and small animals, many of them on the endangered species list. It is a great place for events, birthday parties and school trips. Evie and I love going there. Evie even nagged her parents into allowing her to adopt a penguin called Petal – you pay a certain amount towards the upkeep of your penguin and they send you an owner's certificate, a fact sheet, a free ticket to go and visit, and regular updates about your penguin.

'It's such a shame your mum won't have a bird-table in the garden,' I remark. I am passionate about *all* birds, not just penguins.

'I told you – she's bird-phobic.' Evie's mum has had a fear of birds ever since a starling got into the house and panicked and flew into her face.

'I'd love to see a Golden Oriole,' I sigh. There have been some reported sightings of this rare visitor, and some talk of it breeding in this country now that the weather is warmer, which is really exciting because it is an endangered species.

'Whatever,' says Evie, who is obviously not into Golden Orioles. 'I just wish Mum and Dad would let me have a dog – but they don't want any animals. They're so mean.'

'They let you adopt a penguin. *And* they let you have fish.' Evie has a bowl in her room containing two goldfish called Posh and Pout.

'You can't take them for walks,' Evie grumbles, reluctantly sticking a black footprint on her wallchart.

I sigh and look down at the little patch of lawn at the front of the house – Evie's bedroom looks out on the

POSH AND POUT

street. The lawn is turning brown. There is a hosepipe and lawn-sprinkler ban. Suddenly something catches my eye.

'What's THAT?' I exclaim.

'What?' says Evie. 'Don't tell me you've spotted a Golden wotsit?'

'No! No – it's . . . it's a penguin!'

'Yeah . . . right.'

'No – really – it's a penguin!'

'Put your glasses on, Lola – it's probably a penguin-shaped rock, or something.'

'I told you – I only need the glasses for reading. I don't need them for seeing penguins. And I know a penguin when I see one.'

Evie scrambles over the mound of toys to join me at the window.

'Look – there!'

I point to a small shrub just inside the low wall which separates the garden from the street. Sheltering beside it is what appears to be a very small grey snowman wearing a black hoodie. But unless climate change has gone completely mad, it is not a snowman. It is definitely . . . A PENGUIN!

Chapter Two

Evie and I look at the penguin in the garden and then we look at each other. 'WHY?' we both say.

'I . . . I . . . I don't understand!' I stammer.

Then Evie takes charge of the situation. She likes taking charge. 'What on EARTH is a live penguin doing in my garden?' she exclaims. 'Climate change must be a lot worse than I thought if penguins are turning up in people's gardens! Come on – let's rescue it! Bring a pillowcase!'

'Pillowcase?'

'Yes, we can drape it over the penguin so it doesn't get alarmed – like putting a cloth over a parrot cage.'

Evie's parents have gone shopping, and Liam is engrossed in his latest computer game – Horrible Assassin 2 – so there is no one to question us about why we are rushing out of the front door with a pillowcase.

'Slow down,' hisses Evie. 'We don't want to alarm it. Oh – look! It's *sooo* cute!'

'Are you sure this isn't a dream?' I ask in a hushed

voice. 'Weird things happen in dreams, like penguins suddenly appearing . . . ouch!' Evie has just pinched me.

'You're not dreaming,' she says, as we very slowly approach the penguin.

The penguin doesn't look alarmed – it looks dazed. It doesn't move as we crouch down beside it.

'Oh, I do hope it's not injured!' I whisper.

'It doesn't look injured . . .'

'Who's going to pick it up?'

Evie takes the pillowcase. 'I am,' she says, sounding a little nervous. 'I've always wanted to p— , p— , pick up a penguin. I hope it doesn't peck me!'

Very gently, Evie covers the penguin with the pillow-case and lifts it up.

'Uh-oh – it's struggling! Quick – back to my room!'

Safely back in Evie's room, we carefully unwrap the penguin. Its beak is wide open, probably in alarm, and it waddles and stumbles across the bedroom floor. It looks hot and bothered.

'Open the door of the mini-fridge – we could sit it next to the fridge to cool down,' I suggest.

'I don't want to stress it out,' Evie replies. 'We probably shouldn't keep handling it. Wow! My very own *real* penguin! This is awesome!'

'Yes – but you can't keep it!'

'I *know*! The thing is, I think I recognise it! It's the penguin chick from the Eco Gardens. It had its picture in the paper because it was the first Adelie penguin chick bred in captivity for several years. I even remember they called him Pablo!'

'But how do you know it's Pablo?'

'Because he's got a big white spot on the back of his head, and most Adelie penguins have completely black heads. So he's really unusual!'

I look closely at Pablo. Apart from the white spot, the rest of his head and back are black and he has white rings around his eyes. He keeps opening his short beak.

'Why is he doing that?' I ask.

'He's probably hot – or he may be hungry,' Evie replies.

Neither of us can take our eyes off the penguin.

'How on earth did he end up in Frog Street, anyway?' Evie continues. 'Come on, Lola! Why are we just sitting here? I'll contact the Eco Gardens – I'll ring them – they must be worried sick. Go and get Pablo some water – oh, and a tin of sardines, in case he's hungry!'

Evie can be a *tiny* bit bossy sometimes, but I put up with it when it's in a good cause, like now.

I find Liam in the kitchen, raiding the fridge.

'Hi,' he says, flicking back his long dark fringe and grinning at me.

I feel incredibly hot – it must be the effect of global warming.

'Er, hi!' I reply. 'Do you have any sardines?' It seems an odd thing to say. Liam must think I'm odd. I *feel* odd.

'I think there's a tin in the cupboard. Help yourself. Why do you want sardines?'

'Um . . . um . . . fish oils! Fish oils – they're good for your brain!'

'Is that so?'

'Yes! They're . . . great! But . . . but I must go!'

Clutching the tin of sardines, a one-and-a-half litre non-recyclable plastic – BAD, VERY BAD – bottle of

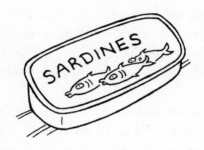

water and the last tattered shreds of my fragile self-esteem – Liam thinks I'm mad – I rush back to Evie's room. Why didn't I just tell him there was a really cute penguin in his sister's bedroom? I think I just felt silly and wanted to escape. Liam might not have believed me. I also wanted to get back to Pablo – he is *soooo* sweet!

'You look really hot,' Evie remarks.

'I *am* hot. Have you spoken to the Eco Gardens?'

'Yes, I've told them we found Pablo in the garden and we're keeping him safe. Someone's going to get back to us in a moment. I left my mobile number.'

Just as she tells me this, her phone rings.

'Yes . . . yes . . . yes . . .' she says, while I do an agitated little dance, wondering what is being said. Pablo has waddled off into a corner and is pecking at one of Evie's soft toys. 'OK,' says Evie, putting down her phone. 'They're coming to get him now. It must be a zillion-to-one chance that he ended up in *my* garden! They've got CCTV footage which shows two youths running away with Pablo, so at least they don't think that *we* took him.'

'That's good!' I exclaim.

'The person I spoke to sounded really grateful – almost close to tears,' says Evie. 'She said they've been having a bad time recently and losing Pablo was the final straw.'

'What sort of bad time?'

'I'm not sure . . . Can I feed Pablo?'

'You can try – I'm not having much luck.'

I have poured some water into an empty pencil tin and pushed it right under Pablo's beak, but he doesn't seem interested. He keeps waddling away. 'How are we going to feed him these sardines?' I ask.

'Parent penguins feed their chicks by regurgitation,' Evie comments. 'So we need to chew up the sardines, swallow them, and then bring them back up . . .'

'Eurgh – gross!' I roll my eyes at her and make a gagging noise.

'OK, maybe not,' she says. 'Why don't we try emptying the sardines into the water?'

She lifts the ring-pull and peels back the lid. A strong smell of sardine fills the room. Pablo opens his beak and lunges at the tin. With a shriek, Evie drops the tin, and water and sardines fly in all directions. Pablo waddles around, gobbling them up. Then he poos.

'Oh – Lola!' Evie exclaims. 'My room's going to *stink*!'

'It's not *my* fault! Do you still want a penguin as a pet? Er, and your mum and dad have just got back with the shopping,' I comment, looking out of the window.

Evie gives another shriek. 'Help! Huge crisis! Mum will go mad if she finds a penguin in the house. She will seriously flip! What are we going to do? Oh, Lola – help!'

It is my turn to take charge. I shoo Pablo as gently as possible into the corner where the great heap of soft toys is piled. He blends in with them and could easily pass as a stuffed penguin as long as he doesn't move, but he seems to be falling asleep anyway. Quickly I cover the white slick of penguin poo with a fluffy pink rug and scoop up the remaining bits of sardine with a handful of tissues and stuff them in the bin, just in time!

We can hear Evie's mum coming up the stairs. 'Yoo-hoo!' she calls. 'We're back!'

Evie looks like a rabbit – or a penguin – caught in headlights. 'I . . . must . . . focus,' she says. 'Stay calm. What would Sherlock Holmes do at a moment of crisis, or when trying to solve a mystery such as a kidnapped penguin turning up in his garden?' We have been reading Sherlock Holmes stories at school – Evie and I are both in Year Eight at Shrubberylands Comprehensive. 'Of course! He'd pick up his violin and play!'

Evie seizes her violin from the open case beside her bed, and draws the bow across the strings just as her mum enters the room.

'Ah! Doing your practice – what a good girl!' says Evie's mum, making a valiant effort not to look pained at the distressed-cat-screeching noises which Evie is wringing out of her instrument.

Evie's mum frowns and wrinkles her nose. 'Why does it smell of fish in here?' she asks.

I see Pablo step forward and I do a quick side step to stand in front of him. Behind me he starts making a strange rasping noise – he has a voice that could grate cheese. I realise that he must have thought that Evie's violin-playing was the sound of another penguin calling to him, and he is answering.

'What's that noise?' Evie's mum asks suspiciously.

'It's my violin, Mum!'

'But I can still hear it, and you're not even playing.'

'It's . . . it's an echo.' Hastily, Evie starts playing again.

Unfortunately, whatever her violin is saying in Adelie-penguin language – perhaps it's a mating call – Pablo responds by barging past my legs and waddling towards her, rasping away.

All hell breaks loose. Evie's mum screams louder than I have ever heard a mother scream before, and Evie's dad and Liam come charging up the stairs.

'Whatever's going on?' her dad demands, bursting into the room. 'What . . . what on earth is a live penguin doing in here?'

'He's not doing any harm!' Evie protests. 'Stop scaring him!'

Evie's mum flees downstairs. It takes a little while to explain the situation to Evie's dad. Liam is fascinated.

'Now I know why you wanted those sardines! Why didn't you say?' he asks me.

'Er . . .' Probably because I seem to be incapable of saying anything except 'er'.

'Hello, little fellow!' says Liam gently, crouching down. 'Are you still hungry? There's some nice fresh fish over here . . .'

'Leave Posh and Pout alone!' Evie exclaims indignantly.

'Stop it, Liam,' says her dad. 'So the people from the Eco Gardens will be here soon to collect him, will they?'

'Yes, Dad. They're on their way.'

'You've done the right thing. Well done, both of you.'

'Thanks, Dad.'

In the pause that follows, we hear Evie's mum calling in a strange, strangled voice from the bottom of the stairs. 'Get . . . that . . . penguin . . . out . . . of . . . here!'

From the street we hear the familiar jingle of Meltonio's Marvellous Mouth-watering Eco-friendly Ices as Meltonio's specially-adapted battery-powered van trundles slowly past our house. Meltonio is our friend – he is just as passionate about green causes as we are.

'Oh, good!' Liam exclaims. 'Ice-cream! It's so hot – I seriously need to chill!'

Suddenly, inspiration strikes me. 'We could ask Meltonio to keep Pablo in his van until the Eco Gardens people get here. It's nice and cool in the van – good for penguins.'

'And good for Mum because the penguin would be out of the house. Brilliant, Lola! You go and ask – I'll bring Pablo.'

Meltonio doesn't understand at first. He thinks that I am offering him a Penguin biscuit, and politely declines as he hands Liam a double-scoop Strawberry Sunrise Sorbet (which is my favourite, too. Liam and I share similar tastes!).

When I explain that the penguin I am talking about is a real one, Meltonio looks worried and says that he is concerned about the Health and Safety implications of having a live penguin in his van. I say that it will probably only be for a few minutes until the Eco Gardens people arrive. Then Evie comes out of the house with Pablo wrapped in the pillowcase, looking *reeeally* cute, and Meltonio relents – he has a soft spot for all animals and birds. His droopy black moustache ripples as his face creases into a big smile.

'Poor little guy!' he says gently. 'I will put him next to the freezer until his owners get here. I can disinfect the van afterwards.'

I can see Mrs Fossett from across the road craning her neck to see what is going on as she clips her hedge. She is the original nosy neighbour, and is always gossiping with her friends, Mrs Baggot and Mrs Throgmorton. Evie and I refer to them, in private, as the Three Witches. Mum told me off about this until they complained about our overgrown hedge and said it lowered the tone of the street; she hasn't told me off since.

THE THREE WITCHES

Pablo is pecking at a Mouth-watering Melon Sugar-free Non-Dairy Nice-Ice, which Meltonio is offering him.

'He likes his food!' says Meltonio approvingly. Meltonio also likes his food and is quite round.

We eat our ice-creams and watch Pablo while we wait for the people from the Eco Gardens to arrive. Meltonio sings gently to Pablo, who seems to go into a kind of trance.

'He's enjoying the singing . . .' Evie whispers to me.

'Or else he's not feeling well,' I say, wishing the Eco Gardens people would hurry up.

'Here comes the van!' Evie exclaims, sounding relieved. The Eco Gardens has a fleet of green-coloured vans which run on bio-fuel, made from animal and bird poo from their own enclosures. I learned this at the Education Zone when we visited the Eco Gardens. I am amazed that the van doesn't smell bad at all.

The Principal Keeper introduces herself and tells us that her name is Kate Meadowsweet. She has curly blond hair and a warm smile. She is bursting with gratitude for the safe return of Pablo. The Penguin Keeper, a slim girl called Annie, her hair tied back in a ponytail, wearing the same uniform of green shirt and shorts as Kate, is equally grateful.

Annie carefully lifts Pablo out of Meltonio's van and puts him into a special penguin-carrier in the back of the Eco Gardens' van. She says that he looks fine after his adventure but that he will be given a full health check by their resident vet.

'We take the utmost care of all our animals and birds,' Kate explains. 'So I do hope you won't take any notice of the awful rumours flying around at the moment about the Eco Gardens. There's absolutely no truth in them. I'm afraid there's a really nasty whispering campaign going on.'

'Oh, we wouldn't believe a word of it,' says Evie. 'We *know* how much you care.'

'Good,' says Kate, smiling ruefully. 'We're beginning to think that someone is trying to get us closed down, but we don't know why. One of the worst rumours is that our birds are carrying the bird-flu virus, which is obviously going to worry a lot of people. But it is absolutely NOT true!'

'I saw that rumour in a letter to the local paper,' says Evie's dad, who has come out to join us – her mum is hiding indoors, still presumably in the grip of severe penguinophobia. 'I didn't really take it too seriously, but I'm afraid my colleague on the council, George Pollard-Morris, *did* take it seriously. George is a confirmed hypochondriac, seriously worried by germs, so you may have a visit from the Health and Safety Inspectors. He'll feel that he must do the responsible thing, obviously, since you lease the land for the Eco Gardens from the council.'

'Oh well,' says Kate with a sigh. 'At least they'll find that everything's fine and they'll give us a clean bill of health – as long as we haven't lost so much support in the meantime that we've gone out of business. Our lease is up for renewal, and these rumours couldn't have come at a worse time. I'd really appreciate it if you would keep the news of Pablo's kidnap quiet. It's so easy to distort facts, and we don't need any more bad publicity. If visitor numbers fall or our charitable donations dry up, we may not be able to keep going.'

Evie and I look so horror-struck that Kate gives us both a hug and assures us that everything will be fine. She invites us to come to the Eco Gardens with our families as her guests tomorrow and she invites Meltonio to come and sell his ices there. Kate goes on to say that she can offer us a small reward, but that the Eco Gardens is seriously short of money. Dad tells her not to worry about giving us a reward, but that we will look forward to visiting the Eco Gardens tomorrow.

'Oh, thank you,' says Kate. 'I feel like a pelican at the moment – no matter which way I turn, there's always a large bill in front of my face!'

Before she and Annie drive away with Pablo, Kate apologises for the fact that we will have a visit from the police later on. She explains that it is just a formality, meaning that they have to ask questions and fill in forms – but we are not under suspicion, Kate will make sure of that. They just want to catch the people who *really* took Pablo.

'My guess is that whoever took him is connected with these rumours,' says Kate. 'They wanted to spread panic by going on about bird flu and then dumping poor Pablo in a public place to frighten people. But for whatever reason, they abandoned him in your garden. Luckily for us.'

We all wave as the green eco-van drives away.

'Phew! What a day!' exclaims Evie, tossing her red curls and kicking off her sky-blue Ethletic canvas boots which are Fair Trade footwear made with sustainably-tapped natural rubber (I am seriously envious of Evie for owning a pair, but Mum says they're too expensive – it must help to have a dad who works in a bank, and a mum who stocks them in her shop.) 'The police were nice, weren't they?'

'Yes – they obviously believed us. I wish we could help them catch the people who took Pablo.'

'We WILL help them,' says Evie firmly. 'And we WILL find out who's spreading those evil rumours. And we WILL save the Eco Gardens!' She sounds very confident for someone who likes to make lists of Things to Worry About.

'Yes,' I agree. 'Eco-worriers will triumph!' I also have my confident moments – as well as my despairing ones.

'And now,' says Evie, standing in front of her eco-wallchart, 'I think that rescuing a penguin from the garden deserves at least three green stars. And I'm going to switch off my mini-fridge *now* – so that's another green star. We'll just have to borrow Liam's old CD player for the moment – I can't *not* listen to Dodo!'

'We'd better finish off the two smoothies that are left,' I say, opening the fridge door. 'And then I'm going home to find out if Mum's gone organic, like I asked her to.'

Before I leave, I ask to borrow *Green Teen* magazine to read tonight – Evie always passes her copy on to me as she is a subscriber.

'I can't wait for tomorrow!' I say.

'Neither can I,' Evie agrees. 'The Eco Gardens are so cool! We *must* help to save them!'

'I agree completely,' I say. 'Try not to worry . . .' I

know this is a pointless thing to say to an eco-worrier –
but we always try to stop each other worrying, even
though we usually succeed in making each other worry
even more.

Chapter Three

Green Teen magazine always gives me plenty to worry about. One outstandingly startling fact catches my eye as I walk from Evie's house back to my own house, which is just two doors away along Frog Street. The fact is so startling that it causes me to trip over next-door's cat. Because it is printed in bold black letters on a yellow background, I can see it without my glasses.

Eco-fact Number Forty-two:

Each year, twenty-eight million tonnes of rubbish is dumped in landfill sites in the UK. This weighs the same as three and a half million double-decker buses, a queue of which would go round the world two and a half times.

Phew! I wonder who worked that one out? *Green Teen* magazine likes to publish these random facts, which tend to stick in my brain. It makes me feel strange, thinking about all that rubbish, and I pass the information on in a text to Evie, in case she somehow managed to miss it, so that she can add it to her latest list of Things to Worry About. I make a mental note to recycle more, and I must remind Mum to put more food peelings, egg-shells, etc. on the compost heap as it means fewer trips to the wheelie-bin and therefore less rubbish. Mum says that I can do it as she is too busy to sort out rubbish – thanks, Mum!

Almost as worryingly, I arrive home to find that Mum has dyed her hair blond – it used to be purest mouse, like mine. I find her in the bathroom, looking into the mirror with a slight frown and running her fingers through her hair, which is still wet and the same colour as straw. My own hair stands on end when I see what she has been using to dye her hair.

'Mum!' I exclaim, picking up the empty packet of dye from the bathroom floor. 'Don't you realise that this product contains bleach? It is *so* bad for the environment. Why didn't you use organic lemon juice? Better for the environment and better for your hair.' Not only is bleach bad for the environment, it is also bad for me to be seen with a mum with weird bleached hair.

Mum shakes her head so that drops of water fly over me – I hope she washed all the bleach out!

'What do you think?' she asks. 'Does it suit me?' She looks so worried that I decide that the words 'old' and

MY OWN HAIR STANDS ON END WHEN
I SEE WHAT SHE HAS BEEN USING...

'tragic' which have popped unbidden into my mind are probably not the best ones to use. I can't help feeling angry, partly about the bleach and partly about the fact that I *liked* it when Mum and I had the same colour hair – I want my old mum back!

But I force a smile and say, 'It's ... er ... very nice, Mum. It makes you look at least six months younger.'

Mum looks doubtful. 'It'll grow out,' she says. 'Eventually. I wonder what Dad's going to say.'

Dad has gone somewhere in the white van with his two young assistants, to put up a marquee for a birthday party in someone's garden. So I tell Mum all about Pablo and the Eco Gardens and the stupid rumours and how we *must* help. I tell her that we are all invited to visit the Eco Gardens tomorrow.

Mum looks at me open-mouthed. 'You and Evie found a penguin?' she says, wonderingly. 'Now there's something that doesn't happen every day! Yes, Dad and I will come with you – how exciting! I can't believe that any of those rumours can be true. I remember it as such a lovely place, and it wasn't that long ago that we went there.'

I give Mum a big hug and tell her that I love her, with or without bleached hair. But preferably without. I wonder if I can persuade her to wear a hat tomorrow?

I even find it in my heart to forgive her for forgetting – again! – to go organic. She has bought non-organic milk and non-organic fruit and vegetables as usual.

'But Mum,' I protest – even though I have forgiven her, it is my duty as an eco-worrier to worry her – 'organic food is better for your body and for the planet.'

'It's not better for my purse!' Mum retorts. 'Organic stuff is more expensive. You should have seen the price of organic butter. It said on the packet that it came from happy cows roaming free in the Swiss Alps, but I'm afraid I can't afford to support their lifestyle.'

'But non-organic stuff costs the earth – literally,' I argue. 'Would you rather save a few pennies, or save the planet? And it would be much better to buy British butter rather than paying to have it flown in from abroad – think about all those carbon emissions from the aeroplanes carrying things like butter!'

Mum looks thoughtful – perhaps I am getting the message through at last. 'Would you like pizza or a frozen curry?' she asks.

'Mum! Ready-meals are the *worst* thing! All that packaging pollutes the planet.' I read out Eco-fact Number Forty-two from *Green Teen* magazine. 'And ready-meals are stuffed full of salt, hydrogenated fats and all sorts of additives. That's why I can't easily do up my jeans. Do you want me to become obese, Mum?'

'You are in no danger of becoming obese, Lola – not with all the swimming and athletics you do. Would you prefer fish fingers?'

'Are they organic?'

'No, I couldn't find organic fish fingers. I did look, like you asked me to.'

'OK.' It was nice of her to look. 'I suppose I'll have

MY DREAM...

TRACK AND FIELD GOLD MEDAL WINNER!

GOING FOR GOLD IN THE OLYMPICS!

fish fingers. But are they from sustainable fish stocks?'

'Oh for goodness' sake, Lola!' Mum slams the packet of fish fingers on to the kitchen table. 'There! You can read all about them on the packet. All I know is that they're made from fish and probably from fingers – and you are driving me round the bend!'

I decide to keep quiet for a while. I suppose a few non-organic fish fingers won't spoil my dream of becoming fit enough to win gold in the Olympics. I go into the living room, taking a non-organic apple from the fruit bowl – so I have to take it back into the kitchen to wash off the harmful chemicals and pesticides before I eat it. I hope Mum remembered to buy loose rather than pre-packaged apples, like I suggested.

Then I have to fetch my glasses from my room. At last, I curl up on the sofa in the living room with *Green Teen* magazine – bliss! 'Wow!' I exclaim, as another start-ling fact hits me full on:

Eco-fact Number Forty-three:

Plugged-in mobile-phone chargers waste over sixty million pounds every year across the UK. So now is the time to SWITCH OFF. No, not your brain, but anything in your house, such as electrical equip-ment left on standby. So go on! Unplug that mobile charger or switch it off at the wall when not in use!

I immediately leap across the room to switch off the television, which has been left on standby as usual. How many times have I told Mum and Dad to turn it off properly? They never listen! Moments later I have to leap across the room to turn it on again as it is time for *Saturday Night Live Jive*, which I enjoy.

Dad arrives home and flops down in his favourite armchair. He looks tired.

'Hi, Dad! Hard day?'

'Hello, love! Yes – hard work. How was your day?'

I start telling him about Pablo. He looks amazed and interrupts me to say that he heard about the kidnapping of the penguin on the local radio news bulletin as he was driving home.

'Oh no!' I exclaim. 'Kate didn't want any publicity . . . Who on earth could have told the radio station about it? Probably the same person who's spreading the rumours. That's so unfair! Did they say we'd rescued the penguin?'

'No, love. They just said that the Ecological Gardens had been experiencing problems and that the council was concerned about the welfare of the animals. Then they simply said that the penguin had been returned, apparently unhurt.'

I am seething with indignation and my hand shakes as I text the news to Evie. She texts me back to say how awful it is. Poor Kate!

Mum comes into the room, nervously adjusting her newly-blond hair. She has brought Dad a drink – a strong one, I think.

'Your . . . hair!' Dad exclaims, visibly shaken. At least Mum's hair now matches Dad's own hair, which is straw-coloured, apart from the greyish bits. It is short and receding slightly. He has the same brown eyes as me, and at the moment they have a startled look in them as he gazes at Mum's hair.

'Er . . . yes. It'll settle down in a few days, I expect,' Mum says.

Dad takes a large sip of his drink and seems to recover his composure. 'It . . . it . . . it's different,' he says. 'I like it! I've never had a blonde wife before . . . er . . . er, you know what I mean!'

We all burst out laughing, and everyone relaxes. My parents are great, even if they're sometimes as uncool as a non-organic cucumber, with a pronounced tendency to behave in an ecologically-unsound way. But I will manage to convert them one day – it is my mission! And my other mission is to help to save the Eco Gardens. But first things first.

'Dad?' I say.

'Yes, love?'

'Is it OK if I put a brick in the cistern in the loo?' Something I have read in *Green Teen* magazine has given me this idea.

Dad frowns. 'Why on earth would you want to do that? Don't you have anything better to do?'

I explain that putting a brick in the cistern cuts down on water consumption and helps to save the world. 'You waste nine litres of water every time you flush the loo,' I explain. 'Putting a brick in the cistern means you save three.' Dad looks doubtful. I tell him that it will reduce his water bill. Dad brightens – his whole attitude changes!

'In that case, go ahead!' he says. 'There's a few old bricks lying around in the back garden.'

ECO-WORRIER INSPIRATION!

Eureka! I have found the winning formula. Dad will agree to almost anything if it saves him money. When I tell him that installing a water butt in the garden will save him even more money, he says that he will give it serious consideration. But I'm not totally convinced that he will get round to it – given a choice between saving the planet and watching television, Dad would probably decide that saving the planet can wait.

* * *

Before I go to bed, I send a message to Evie reminding her to switch off her mobile charger, and to ask her what time it is that we are supposed to arrive at the Eco Gardens. She texts back to say that we are expected there at ten in the morning, and that she has already switched off her mobile charger, but that she will have to switch it on again and charge her phone if she has to send me many more messages.

Moments later, I get another message from Evie to say that she will be round early tomorrow morning and that she can't stop thinking about Kate and the report on the radio station, and that she would like to come to the Eco Gardens with me and my parents because she doesn't want to roll up with her family in their seriously non-eco-friendly gas-guzzling 4x4. I am not sure that our old white van is much better. I have a sneaky suspicion that Mum and Dad will suggest that we all go in the 4x4.

After a few minutes, I get another message from Evie to say that her family is driving her mad, and she can't wait to see me in the morning. She says she feels too hot to sleep. I send a message back advising her to do some simple toning and stretching exercises which I try to do every evening as it helps to tire me out – sometimes I feel too awake at night. But not tonight – I feel tired . . .

Finally, as I am drifting off to sleep, I get yet *another* message from Evie to say that the exercises have made her even hotter and now she is going to have to charge her phone again, and she feels bad about this and will therefore have to stick a black footprint on her eco-chart.

Sometimes I think that Evie worries *too* much . . . Although I suppose I should follow the example she set by turning off the mini-fridge in her room by turning off the sparkly fairy lights in my room which are burning up unnecessary electricity.

I fall asleep and dream of myself winning a gold medal in the pole vault at the Olympics, and then, even more bizarrely, I dream of Pablo winning the star prize on *Saturday Night Live Jive*.

Eco-fact Number Five:

Many fish stocks are moving northward in search of cooler waters. Fish stocks that used to stay in Cornwall have moved as far north as the Shetland Islands.

Chapter Four

Eco Gardens Day!

As she said she would, Evie arrives early on Sunday morning while I am still in bed. She seems to be in high spirits and jumps on to the bed, her red curls bouncing up and down.

'Evie! I'm still asleep!' I protest, trying to pull my duvet over my face, although the thought that we are off to the Eco Gardens today sends a little rush of excitement through me.

'So wake up!' she says cheerily. 'I don't know why I'm so wide awake. I couldn't sleep last night because I was too worried and hot. But today's the day we can start trying to find out who's spreading those rumours, and then maybe we can help. AND we're going to see Pablo, AND Petal, the penguin I adopted! I wonder if either of them will recognise us?'

'I wonder if you could stop bouncing?' I ask, giving her a friendly push.

'Sorry,' she says. 'It's such a relief to be here, away from my annoying family.' She stops bouncing. 'Your mum's gone blonde,' she adds, as an afterthought.

'I *know*. Couldn't she just have looked *normal* for our visit to the Eco Gardens? And she used *bleach*. I told her she should have used organic lemon juice.'

'Really? That's interesting. Do you think it would work on my freckles? I'm fed up with having a frecklefest for a face.'

'No, don't. Don't change a thing – I like you the way you are.'

Evie grins at me. 'Thanks, Lola!'

'So why were your family annoying you?' I ask, brushing my hair and wondering vaguely what I would look like as a blonde.

'Oh, don't ask!' exclaims Evie, rolling her eyes. 'But I'll tell you. Dad was really annoying me – he just sat in front of the television all evening, despite me telling him about all the easy-to-do jobs he could be getting on with during these long summer evenings, such as insulating the loft. I read about it in the green guide. It would help to reduce our energy consumption by stopping all that heat escaping through the roof, and so our total carbon footprint would get smaller.'

'What did your dad say?'

'He just gave me a strange look and went back to watching the television.'

'Try telling him it would save him money. That always works with my dad.'

Evie nods.

'So what happened after that?' I ask.

'Oh, I fell out with Liam. He keeps saying he's too busy to teach me to play the guitar. It's not true – he just can't be *bothered*. Then he played on his electric drums for hours – *thud thud thud* – right under my room. It was driving me mad. So I told him off for using too much electricity. And he said that was a good reason for not teaching me the electric guitar! He said it was boring the way I go on about global warming all the time, and told me to go away. So I switched off his phone charger and his laptop, which he'd left on. He wasn't very pleased. Later on I told him off for using an electric toothbrush and leaving the water running while he was brushing his teeth. Leaving the tap running wastes over six litres of water a minute! So he said if I was that bothered, why didn't I share his bathwater? He even offered to save it for me next time he has a bath. I mean – yuck! Totally gross! He cuts his toenails in the bath.'

Although I like Liam, this last detail is straying into the realms of too much information. 'And what about your mum? Was she annoying you, too?'

'Yes! Guess what? I found that the freezer in the garage has been running with nothing but a two-year-old pizza and a few pork chops in it for months. Talk about wasteful! I had a go at her about that – AND I had to stick a whole handful of black footprints on my eco-chart because of my stupid family!'

'Hmm,' I say again. 'I wonder if having a go at your

family is the best approach? Perhaps a little gentle per-suasion would work better?'

'You may be right.' Evie chews her bottom lip and twists one of her red curls round and round her finger. 'I suppose I was a bit harsh. Maybe I should go back and make peace.'

'Good idea. I'll come with you.' Quickly I pull on my white shorts and a green T-shirt as it is another hot day. Then I decide to do a few warm-up exercises – touching my toes, followed by a quick burst of star-jumps. Evie is

A SUDDEN BURST OF
STAR-JUMPS !

wearing white cropped trousers and the brown organic cotton T-shirt which she found at Green Aid, the local charity shop where Evie and I find numerous bargains. Evie is proud of her mum's shop, Fashion Passion, as it promotes ethical shopping and stocks Ethletic trainers, among other items, but it is very expensive.

'Come on!' Evie says. 'Stop doing your exercises – you make me feel so unfit! We've got about half an hour until it's time to go . . .'

'Oh, by the way,' I say. 'Mum phoned your mum and asked if we could all go in the 4x4.'

'I *know*!' groans Evie.

Out in Frog Street we see the neighbour's cat, Boris, and can't resist stopping to stroke him – he is a big friendly black cat who winds around our legs and has a strangely high-pitched miaow.

'Why don't we go swimming together soon?' I suggest.

BORIS THE CAT

'Cats don't swim,' Evie replies.

'No, idiot!' I say, laughing. 'I meant *you* – not Boris! You can help me get in shape for the Olympics – swimming's one of the best forms of exercise. And it would be fun. We used to go swimming together all the time when we were little.'

As we are making a fuss of Boris the cat, Mrs Fossett walks past with her friends, Mrs Baggot and Mrs Throgmorton. They are gossiping, as usual.

'That place is a disgrace, Enid,' says Mrs Fossett.

'Oh, I agree, Betty. It should be closed down immediately! I heard that two of the parrots died of flu last week, but it was all hushed up.'

'Disgraceful!' barks Mrs Thorgmorton. 'Fancy having somewhere like that so close to where we live. This is a respectable place – we don't want bird flu. They should rename it the Biological Hazard Gardens!'

'Millicent! You are a hoot!' shrieks Mrs Baggot.

Evie and I exchange horrified looks. 'They're talking about the Eco Gardens – the old witches,' whispers Evie.

Anger bubbles up inside me. 'It's not true!' I call out after them. 'You shouldn't listen to rumours.' I notice that Evie's face has flushed red with furious indignation beneath her freckles.

The Three Witches turn their heads to look at us as if we are out-of-control hooligans in need of stern discipline. I stare back.

Evie turns away, muttering, 'Maybe they *started* the rumours.'

Then Mrs Fossett sniffs loudly and turns her back on us, exclaiming, 'Well – really!' Mrs Baggot and Mrs Throgmorton follow her, making loud remarks about 'young people today'.

'Just wait till I'm a teenager,' I hiss. 'Ha ha! They must be dreading *that*!'

Evie giggles. 'Come on!' she says. 'Don't let them spoil our day.'

Evie's mum and dad and Liam are all in the kitchen having breakfast. The radio is on and a song called 'Don't Worry, Be Happy!' is playing. I give the radio an evil look – although I realise that it is not the fault of the radio itself that the rumours about the Eco Gardens and Pablo's kidnapping were broadcast yesterday on the Shrubberylands FM news bulletin.

Evie clears her throat and says, rather awkwardly, 'Er, I'm sorry if I was a pain yesterday.'

'You're a pain every day,' remarks Liam, who doesn't look properly awake yet. His dark hair is tousled and I get a strange wobbly jelly feeling in my stomach. Then I remember Evie's remark about his toenail clippings in the bath, and the feeling passes.

'Be quiet, Liam,' says Evie's mum. 'That's OK, love. We all know you're at a difficult age.'

How embarrassing. I can sense Evie seething at having her concern for the environment put down to the state of her hormones. I can't help wondering if Evie's mum is also at a 'difficult age' – she has the same mass of red curls as Evie, but for some reason today she has tied little colourful ribbons into them.

'Your hair looks strange, Mum,' says Evie, bluntly – she is annoyed.

Her dad saves the day by telling her that he has been thinking about what she said about insulating the loft, and he is intending to log on to a loft insulation website very soon, and conduct proper research into the subject.

'That's . . . er . . . great, Dad. But if we could just get on and do it, I'd be willing to help.'

'I know you would, love. Now – we'd better get ready to go.' He turns to Evie's mum. 'Are you sure you'll be all right, dear? You know there are a lot of birds at the Eco Gardens.'

'I know. But I've got to get on top of this phobia. I'm OK with birds really – as long as they don't come in the house!'

The doorbell rings. Mum and Dad have arrived, and it is time for us all to pile into the Revro Widespace 4x4. Liam seems grumpy, and sits in the back, listening to music on his iPod.

'Why's Liam in a mood?' I whisper to Evie.

'Oh, he can't think of a name for his new band,' she replies.

I can see that Evie's mum is fascinated by Mum's hair. They have been friends for a long time, having met and immediately got on well when Evie and I were at primary school together. Evie's mum says that she likes Mum's hair, and suggests that she drops in at Fashion Passion soon to look for some clothes to go with her new look. Then they start giggling together about something. So now I'm going to be turning up at the Eco Gardens in a gas-guzzling Monster Truck with a couple of giggling mothers with unusual hair.

But as long as I have my fellow eco-worrier with me, I don't mind. Nothing can stop us having the BEST day . . .

The Revro Widespace seems huge as Evie's dad manoeuvres it into a space beside the fleet of green Eco Gardens bio-fuel vans.

'I'm never coming here in this again!' Evie whispers to me.

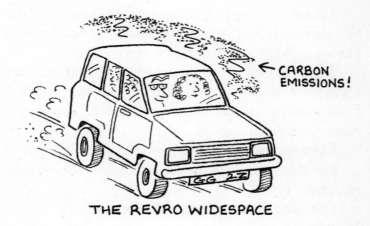

CARBON EMISSIONS!

THE REVRO WIDESPACE

'Me neither,' I agree. 'Can't you persuade your dad to trade it in for something that runs on poo or some kind of renewable fuel? You got him to agree to insulate the loft.'

'I'll try,' says Evie. 'But all he ever does when I suggest

anything is research it on the internet. And that means he's just using up even *more* energy, using the computer.'

'And of course downloading cute pictures of cuddly penguins and printing them out is *really* helping the environment,' remarks Liam, sarcastically, getting out of the 4x4 behind us.

'Shut up, Liam!' Evie snaps back. 'At least I don't spend most of my waking hours playing Horrible Assassin 2.'

'Sh!' I say. 'Here comes Kate.'

Kate Meadowsweet greets us warmly. She has a large blue parrot perched on her shoulder. He is *sooo* beautiful! I take photos on my camera phone.

'Meet Mr Macawber,' she says, as the parrot – actually a macaw – shuffles down her arm.

'Pleased to meet you,' says Mr Macawber in a strange, strangled, staccato voice.

'Oh – he can talk!' says Mum in delight.

Mr Macawber looks at her out of his yellow-ringed eye. Evie's mum is not looking so delighted. She edges away from Mr Macawber and Evie's dad grips her arm reassuringly.

Kate Meadowsweet smiles. 'He can say a few words,' she says. 'He comes from our new Encounter Village where you can go to get up close and personal with some of our tamer creatures. Let me show you around.' She gives Mr Macawber to another keeper who carries him away, much to Evie's mum's relief. Kate looks around, and

MR MACAWBER

seems suddenly downcast. 'There aren't many visitors so far today and I'm really worried about the news of Pablo's kidnapping getting broadcast on the radio yesterday. The radio station phoned me up and said they'd had an anonymous caller who'd told them about it. There didn't seem to be much point in denying it, so I just said that Pablo was fine now and put the phone down. Perhaps I seemed a bit rude because then they said on the news bulletin that we had "problems" – that may have put people off.'

'I hope you don't think that any of us phoned the radio,' Evie blurts out, voicing what I was thinking.

'Of *course* not!' Kate exclaims. 'I *know* you wouldn't!'

'Good!' Evie and I say together.

'Because we really want to help find out who's spreading the rumours and who took Pablo,' Evie continues.

'Thanks,' says Kate, smiling again. 'I'm so sorry,' she apologises, pulling herself together. 'You're here to see what a big, happy family we are at the Eco Gardens, and here I am being miserable. That won't do at all! It's time to show you what a special place this is.'

Kate shows us an area of carefully-managed woodland beside the car park. 'Trees are so important,' says Kate. 'They take in carbon dioxide, which is one of the greenhouse gases, and give out oxygen. But when trees die, or when they are cut down, like they are in the rainforest, carbon dioxide is released back into the atmosphere – that's why it's so important to stop deforestation and to conserve trees. We love our woodland.'

'I planted two acorns last year,' Evie tells Kate. 'But it will be a while before I have a woodland area as big as this.'

'I bet it's full of birds,' I enthuse, wishing I'd remembered to bring my binoculars.

The woodland is part of the Eco Gardens, but the animals and birds are kept in enclosures in a parkland area which is reached through the main entrance where the payment kiosks are. As we walk down the central path, lined with beautifully kept flower-filled borders, with turnings-off to the various animal enclosures, a dreadful howling surrounds us, as if a hundred screaming banshees are whirling overhead.

'Don't worry!' Kate shouts above the noise. She points to a large caged enclosure to our left. 'Those are our Black Howler Monkeys, Mick and Keith. Their call is nearly ninety decibels, which is *very* loud, as you can hear. We got them just the other day to deter intruders.

They're our largest animals, apart from the gibbons – and they certainly make their presence felt!'

Mick and Keith's howling nearly drowns out another more familiar noise – the jingle of an ice-cream van . . .

'Meltonio!' We run to greet him as he drives very slowly up the path and parks on the grass to one side.

'How's business, Meltonio?' Kate asks.

'It's a little slow, but don't worry! It's a beautiful day – things will pick up!' says Meltonio, as we all crowd round to buy ice-creams.

'He's such a nice man,' says Kate, as we walk away from the van. 'He really wants to help the Eco Gardens, and he's just agreed to pay us a small percentage of his profits from each day he sells his ices here. But he'll end up losing business at this rate.'

Evie nudges my arm and I nearly drop my Strawberry Sunrise Sorbet (I chose it so that Liam would see that I share the same taste in ice-cream as him, but then he chose a Chocolate Dream Superscoop, which looks seriously yummy).

'Look!' exclaims Evie. 'There's Pablo! I can see the white spot on his head. He is *soooo* cute!'

'Wow! Penguins!' I enthuse, as we race over to the penguin pool, our families trailing behind – they seem to be more interested in their ice-creams.

'Welcome to Penguin Paradise,' says Kate, once we have all gathered in a group. 'I'll hand you over to Annie, who will explain some of the special features and answer any questions you may have. Then it will be feeding time.'

Evie links her arm through her mum's. Her mum is looking slightly nervous, but she forces a smile – she is obviously determined to beat her penguinophobia.

'Hi,' says Annie. 'I hope you'll agree that this is paradise – the penguins certainly seem to think it is. The pool is an irregular shape to make the underwater environment more interesting, and you can go down those steps into a tunnel and watch the penguins "flying" like mini torpedoes underwater through special viewing windows. There are rocks and shingle on the "beaches" to provide variety, and specific grasses and plants. Two biological filters clean and purify the water to avoid the use of potentially harmful chemicals, so the penguins' home is definitely "green". It certainly is a pool with a view, as you can see!' Annie indicates the parkland beyond Penguin Paradise.

'Look!' Evie exclaims. 'There's Petal – the penguin I adopted! I know it's her because of her pink tag.'

All the penguins have different coloured tags on their wings so that they can be easily identified. Petal has a pink tag and Pablo has a green one.

'OK, let's get on with feeding time.' Annie fetches a blue bucket full of glistening silver-scaled fish. I see Pablo, on the opposite side of the pool, toboggan down a sloping piece of rock and splash into the water in order to swim across to his breakfast.

'How often do they eat?' Evie's mum asks.

'They have three meals a day. You'll see that I'm stuffing two tablets into the mouth of this fish. One is a vitamin pill, because the penguins' fish comes to us

TOBOGANNING !

frozen, and frozen fish loses vitamins. The other one is a salt tablet because penguins drink saltwater, as all the freshwater in their natural environment is frozen into ice. They can filter the excess salt out of their bills.'

'So that's why Pablo didn't want the freshwater we offered him,' I say.

The penguins crowd round Annie and she throws them handfuls of fish. Some of them are making the same rasping noise that we heard Pablo make.

'They're really fat!' Evie observes, giggling.

'Yes,' agrees Annie, laughing, 'but not too fat. Our penguins are well fed. That's not always the case in the wild – over-fishing means less food for penguins. But the penguins who live here don't have any problems.'

With a last glance back at Pablo and Petal swimming happily with their penguin pals and the Eider ducks who share their pool, we follow Kate back to the main path, which curves around a circular, raised flowerbed full of shrubs. There are benches where visitors can sit and enjoy the tranquillity – except that there aren't many visitors, apart from ourselves. We're so hot that we stop to buy recyclable bottles of water from a drink and snack kiosk.

Kate takes us to the Education Zone, which is next to the gibbon enclosure. Two of the big black gibbons are swinging along a branch inside their cage making a loud WOOH! WOOH! noise.

Inside the Education Zone we see a display of illegally-smuggled items seized by customs officials at Heathrow Airport, which has loaned the items to the Eco Gardens to exhibit. There is a real tiger skin, elephant tusks, the tail of a Bird of Paradise which has been made into a fan, rhino horn, and bags and belts made of crocodile and snake skin, among other things.

'How horrible,' says Evie. 'Why would anyone want to kill such rare and beautiful animals?'

'Some of the animal products are used in oriental medicine,' says Kate. 'I agree it's horrible.'

We wander into another room, where there are life-

HANGING OUT WITH THE GIBBONS

like displays of various eco-disasters, such as a beach covered in an oil slick and several oil-covered dead penguins. Another display shows a wasteland full of litter and various dead animals which have obviously choked on the litter.

In another, more cheerful, room, we are allowed to hold a Giant Thorny Stick Insect in the palms of our hands. We are also offered the chance to hold a Hissing Cockroach but everyone declines apart from Liam, who, according to his sister, has always loved disgusting things.

'That's why I love *you*!' Liam retorts, holding the Hissing Cockroach up to Evie's face. She backs away with a shriek. 'I know how much you love all living things,' he says. 'Wouldn't you like Harry the Hissing Cockroach as a pet? Isn't he just *soooo* cute?'

Evie gives Liam one of her looks, but he doesn't seem worried.

Our next stop is at the Tropical Rainforest Zone, which is in a special building heated by solar panels. A large notice just inside the entrance tells us that an area of rainforest the size of the Eco Gardens is cleared every minute of every night and day.

The Rainforest Zone is full of exotic plants – banana plants, pineapple, papaya, avocado, ginger, vanilla, hibiscus and philodendrons. A spray above our heads sends out the occasional burst of fine mist to keep the air humid. It feels lovely to walk through, and Evie and I just want to stay and feel the mist again! We see butterflies in the same glass enclosures as tiny Arrow Poison Frogs in jewel-like colours, and Liam is fascinated by the Giant Chirping Tree Frog. We are introduced to Dave the Chameleon, who was rescued and given to the Eco Gardens after someone attempted to smuggle him illegally into the country. We also meet Monty the Royal Python, who coils himself around Liam's arm and stares into his face, his tongue flicking in and out.

'That's how snakes smell,' says Kate. 'Through their tongues. He's checking you out, Liam!'

I think Liam is really brave.

Evie points to a big black bird with a yellow breast and blue-rimmed eyes. It is called a Cuvier's Toucan, and

it has a huge red and yellow beak. We stop to watch it happily splashing around in the mud, and Kate explains that the mud helps to get rid of feather mites.

Just outside the Rainforest Zone there is a special glass-fronted enclosure housing some little furry creatures called Rock Hyraxes, which are sprawled luxuriously on specially-heated artificial rocks.

'Liam!' Evie exclaims. 'Why don't you call your band "The Rock Hyraxes"? It's a great name!'

Liam smiles. 'I'll think about it,' he says.

On our way to the Eco-Café which, Kate tells us, serves delicious Fair Trade organic food, we pass keepers with spades and wheelbarrows shovelling dung – mainly

A ROCK HYRAX

from the goats, pigs and chickens at Encounter Village, Kate explains, to use in the Eco Gardens' bio-fuel.

'Now there's something really useful you could do to help the environment!' Liam exclaims. 'My little sister would like to volunteer to help shovel dung,' he says.

Kate grins.

'Shut up, Liam,' hisses Evie, going red in the face.

'I'm sure there are many other ways you can help,' says Kate, kindly.

'Oh, I mean – of course I *would* be prepared to shovel dung if . . . if . . .' Evie stumbles over her words.

'If the alternative was death,' Liam says, completing her sentence for her.

I am torn between a desire to giggle and a need to keep a straight face so that Evie doesn't think I am laughing at her. We are saved from further embarrassment by the sound of a girl shrieking nearby.

'Oh! GROSS!'

We turn to see Amelia Plunkett, who is in our year at school, with her parents and a shaven-headed boy with a pierced eyebrow. He has a thin face, small beady eyes and

MEERKAT

rat-like features. They are standing beside the nearby meerkat enclosure.

'Those awful little rat things are eating those beetles LIVE!' shrieks Amelia. 'That is so, like, totally gross!' She points at the meerkats.

Evie nudges me and we both start giggling. Amelia is not our favourite person. She likes to make fun of us and taunt us for being 'pathetic' and '*soooo* not cool!'. She, on the other hand, considers herself to be coolness personified – but we prefer to think of her as Airhead Amelia, always bringing glossy magazines into school to try to impress people with her superior knowledge about anything to do with celebrities.

'Oh, yuck!' shrieks Amelia again. 'That pig over there just *pooed*!' She points to an enclosure containing rare-breed pigs. 'Can we go home now? I don't like it here. I want to go shopping.'

'OK, darling, let's go,' says her father, who is a short, fat, balding man with a red face. His wife is much taller than he is, wearing a very short yellow skirt and a bright-pink frilly blouse. She totters after her husband and daughter on very high yellow heels, a matching handbag slung over one arm – all the yellow clashes with her dyed blond curls. I realise that compared to Mrs Plunkett, my own mum, in her plain white T-shirt and jeans, looks completely normal – I am even getting used to her hair!

'I wonder why they bothered coming here,' Evie says. 'Look – Amelia's actually trying to flirt with that boy . . . as if he'd be interested in a stupid little girl like her. I think she's seen us – that's why she's trying to look as if she's *with* him! She thinks she's such an expert on relationships.'

'I wish she had a relationship with her brain,' I comment.

'I recognise that boy,' says Liam. 'His name's Dean

Hughes – he was in my year at school. He was always getting into trouble and getting suspended. I can't imagine why he's come here today – it's totally not his scene.'

Kate grins nervously, and we continue on our way to the Eco-Café. When we get there, it is quite empty – the wooden picnic tables dotted around the Gardens have all been empty too. There is one person serving, and all sorts of delicious food and drinks on offer. The pale-green walls are covered in large posters proudly proclaiming that the milk used in the Eco-Café is locally-sourced, while the Fair Trade Arabica coffee beans come from Guatemala.

Evie and I have organic raspberry smoothies and a flapjack each, and are fascinated to see our parents and Liam thoroughly enjoy their first ever totally organic lunch – vegetable lasagne and bean salad. Will they be converted to an organic diet?

'Talk about wind power,' says Liam quietly to Evie afterwards. 'I thought we were trying to cut down on emissions. But after all those beans, I'm not sure I can.'

Evie groans and covers her face with her hands. But Kate, who has overheard, starts rocking with laughter.

All too soon it is time to say goodbye and thank you to Kate – and goodbye to Meltonio, and Mr Macawber, who has been brought back to see us go.

Evie and I sing 'Change the World' – Dodo's chart-topping eco-rock ballad – at the tops of our voices in the 4x4 going home, until Liam interrupts us with a brilliant impression of Amelia, shrieking, 'OH! LIKE TOTALLY GROSS! THAT PIG JUST POOED!' in a silly, high-pitched voice. Everyone laughs, and I can't stop giggling. The day has got even hotter and I am trying not to be grateful for the air-conditioning in the 4x4 as I know how non eco-friendly it is. I imagine a black carbon footprint hovering above us. But it *is* lovely and cool in the 4x4.

Evie asks if I can stay at her house tonight so that we can plan how we are going to help Kate to save the Eco Gardens. I say, 'Oh, *pleeease!*' I am bubbling over with all the bright and beautiful things I have seen today – all those wonderful birds, including lovebirds, hummingbirds, honey-creepers, kookaburras and Chris the Rhea, who is a large ostrich-like bird – a bird-lover's heaven on earth! I have so many amazing memories and images on my phone to share with Evie tonight.

CHRIS THE RHEA

'And we need to find out who's spreading those rumours,' says Evie. 'Can we look on the council website when we get back, Dad? I want to make sure the council isn't taking the rumours seriously, since they lease the land to Kate. Could the council make trouble for Kate, Dad?'

Evie's dad replies that he thinks it's very unlikely that this would happen, but that the council could refuse to renew the lease if it felt that there were serious problems.

'But you're on the council, Dad – you could reason with them.'

Evie's mum tells us not to worry. She is in a very good mood because she has managed to keep her bird phobia under control. She tells us that she really liked the love-birds and the fat little quail – and Mr Macawber. But I have a feeling that she is relieved to be going home.

Mum and Dad say that it's fine for me to stay with Evie tonight. Evie cheers up. We always enjoy our Eco-worriers' Nights In.

'We can eat the chocolate I bought in the Eco Gardens' gift shop,' I say.

'Shame on you!' says Liam. 'Think of all those air miles and carbon emissions flying cocoa beans round the world to make your chocolate. And you'll get spots!'

'Ignore him!' says Evie. 'He's only jealous because he's not invited.'

Typical Eco-worriers' Night In (brothers not allowed)
1) Listen to music.
2) Gossip.
3) Worry. Make new plan to save world.
4) Eat biscuits, chocolate, etc. – preferably organic. Drink smoothies – or water.
5) Worry about eating unhealthy food.

6) Reassure each other.
7) Have pillowfight.
8) Beauty sleep. ZZZZ . . .

Eco-fact Number Six:

A cow produces five hundred litres of methane per day in its burps and farts. (Even the most flatulent human only produces one and a half litres per day.) Livestock such as cows, sheep and pigs produce 2.7 billion tonnes of greenhouse gas every year, which is one fifth of all emissions.

Chapter Five

'And *that would* certainly result in the destruction of the penguins' habitat; as Annie was saying,' I add, after reading the above fact aloud to Evie.

'I don't think you should read while walking down the stairs,' says Evie. 'Especially since you haven't got your glasses on!'

We are on our way to the kitchen to get a drink each to take back to Evie's room. Evie's mum is in the kitchen chatting with her friend, Wanda, who has just dropped in. Wanda works for the local paper, *The Shrubberylands Sentinel* – I wonder if she would give the Eco Gardens a good write-up and say that the rumours aren't true. *The Shrubberylands Sentinel* is a very popular weekly paper which follows stories of local and sometimes even national importance as they unfold. But Wanda and Evie's mum are deep in conversation, and I don't like to interrupt.

'Oh, yum! Organic smoothies in recyclable bottles!' exclaims Evie, peering into the fridge. 'And Liam hasn't found them yet – cool!'

It is a hot and humid evening – it feels stormy – so I ask for a glass of water as well.

'On the subject of water,' says Evie, handing me a glass. 'I've been on at Dad to get a water butt to collect rainwater to use on the garden, but he *still* hasn't. Even Mrs Fossett's got one. You can see it through the kitchen window, just to the side of her house – see? Mrs Fossett's got a huge butt!'

'Don't be rude, Evie,' says her mum, who has been only half-listening.

'It's true!' Evie insists. 'Mum, why hasn't Dad got a water butt yet? And since he's on the council, it should be easy enough for him to get planning permission to put a wind turbine on the roof. Then we could generate our own electricity, and Dad would save loads of money as well as the world. Isn't it time we started being more eco-friendly?'

Evie's mum sighs. 'If I were you, love, I'd leave Dad alone for a while. He's already agreed to insulate the loft. Couldn't we have a break from all the eco-stuff? I know you mean well, but Dad and I get a bit weary after a hard day's work, and we're more inclined to flop in front of the telly rather than go out and save the world. And you upset Dad a bit when you told him to trade in the 4x4 for a more fuel-efficient model with lower emissions. You know how proud he is of his Revro Widespace.'

It is Evie's turn to sigh. 'I'm not going to give up,' she says, stubbornly.

There is a short pause. I pluck up courage – it is now or never.

'Er . . . Wanda?'

'Yes?' Wanda looks surprised – I haven't really spoken to her before.

'You know the Ecological Gardens?'

'Yes, I've been hearing all about your visit there today. I was really surprised to hear how good it sounds after what I've been hearing on the radio and elsewhere. We've been getting letters at the *Sentinel* about fears of bird flu and other problems at the Eco Gardens.

'Oh, *pleeease* don't take them seriously!' I beg. 'Someone's trying to spread these awful rumours to make trouble and now they're losing visitors, and it's not fair because they care passionately about all their creatures and . . . and could you give them a really good write-up in your paper and tell everyone to ignore these rumours because they are *so* not true?' I stop, feeling slightly breathless.

Evie is nodding agreement. 'That's such a good idea, Lola! Oh, *pleeease*, Wanda! Could you do that? Oh, and we could write a letter to the paper, too, to say that the rumours aren't true.'

Wanda looks taken aback. Then she smiles. 'It's not the sort of thing I normally do,' she replies. 'I'll have to talk to my editor first. And I'm afraid that I don't have the final say over which letters are chosen to be published.'

'But you'll see what you can do?' Evie persists.

'Certainly,' Wanda agrees.

'Let's go and log on to the council website,' says Evie. 'I want to make sure the council isn't going to start taking these rumours seriously.'

'You know I don't like chat rooms,' says Evie's mum.

'MUM! It's the *council*! People go on it to talk about wheelie-bins and waste disposal. The only danger we're likely to be in is of being bored to death! Come on, Lola!'

We meet Liam on the stairs. He is on his way out and has been spraying himself liberally with bodyspray. It is very strong – but I like it.

'Wow, Liam! How many cans of bodyspray have you used?' asks Evie.

'What do you want me to do? Smell?' Liam retorts. 'Oh, that's right. You want me to give up baths to save water.'

'No – I never said that!' Evie says.

'I've got another good idea to save water,' Liam continues. 'I remember you telling me that you use nine litres of water every time you flush the loo. But dogs just use a lamppost – they don't waste *any* water.'

'Liam, I don't know quite what you're suggesting . . .'

'I'm suggesting you use a lamppost and save water!'

'OH, GROSS! You are the most disgusting brother EVER! Please – go away!'

I am giggling so much that I nearly spill my drink. Evie drags me off to her room, where she logs on to the council website. Meanwhile I get out the organic chocolate truffles which I bought at the Eco Gardens' gift shop. I also bought a cuddly flamingo and a pencil made from recycled polystyrene cups from the wide range of zoo-venirs on offer. Evie bought a cuddly penguin keyring and another wallchart – this one shows all the different varieties of dolphins and porpoise. It is going to have to join the other posters on the ceiling as there is no room anywhere else.

'I've found the council website,' says Evie. 'Now, what should I click on? Presumably not "Waste Disposal". How about "Your Say" – that sounds more like it.' I offer her an organic truffle. 'Go and get Liam's portable CD player from his room, Lola – I feel in need of some Dodo. I've put the Koolsounds mini-fridge in the garage so I'm not tempted to use it.'

'Won't Liam mind me going in his room?'

'He won't know – he's gone out, hasn't he?'

Feeling rather nervous – what if he suddenly comes

ORGANIC
CHOCOLATE
TRUFFLES
FAIRTRADE

back? – I creep into Liam's room. It is even more of a jumbled mess than Evie's room, except that there are several guitars leaning against the wall and the unmade bed – the drums are downstairs in the garage. There are several cans of Bodyblitz Bodyspray lying on the bed. It smells nice . . .

'LOLA! Come here!' Evie's voice makes me jump violently. Seizing the portable CD player, I hurry back.

'What is it? What have you found?' I ask.

'Look at this,' says Evie. 'It's really bad.'

Peering at the screen (I have left my glasses at my house), I read what it says.

Whisperer: The Eco Gardens is contaminated by the bird-flu virus. Birds are dying every day, but they're trying to hush it up so that they can get more of your money. Ignore me at your peril! I am the Whisperer.

'Isn't it awful?' Evie says in an anguished voice.

'It's bad,' I agree. 'But the council website is so boring – surely not many people are going to see it?'

'Apart from the council people themselves, and they *do* matter,' Evie answers. 'They could close the place down. We've got to do something, Lola! We've got to find out who it is, and we've got to stop them. First of all, I'm going to add our voice to the website – we need to tell people that the Whisperer is lying. What name shall we use?'

'Eco-worrier?'

'Yes – and what shall we say?'

'Say that there's no truth in the rumours and that no birds have died and that the Eco Gardens is the best place to visit if you want to see happy, healthy birds and animals.'

'That should do it.' Evie adds our message to Your Say. 'There. I hope that stops the stupid Whisperer in their tracks.'

'I wish we knew who it was,' I say, putting on our favourite Dodo CD.

'It's probably Mrs Fossett and her friends,' says Evie, standing up and stretching, before going over to the window and looking out. It is oppressively hot, and strange towering clouds are rolling up from the horizon.

'Does Mrs Fossett even have a computer?'

'Yes. Dad had to go and help her to set it up and use it. She got it in order to email her son in Australia. I expect he went to Australia to get away from her!'

'So it *could* be her.'

'Yes. I'm trying to see into her front room – she might be sitting at the computer right now. But I can't really see from here.'

'Wait a minute! Didn't I leave my binoculars here the other day? When I was watching the swifts from your room?'

'Yes – they're under the bed. Good idea. Give them here.'

Evie leans out of the window and trains the binoculars on Mrs Fossett's house.

'I can see something . . . I think it's her . . . she's moving round the room . . . she's making a phone call . . .'

I hear a phone ring somewhere in the house.

Evie's mum shouts up the stairs, 'Evie! Mrs Fossett says would you please stop watching her through binoculars. Would you behave, please? Or Lola will have to go home.'

Evie sits down on her bed. 'So that didn't work,' she says. 'But I still think it might be her.'

'Whoever it is has just posted another message on the website,' I say. Evie comes over to look.

```
Whisperer: Don't listen to Freako-
warrior. They are trying to fool you.
They are an agent for the forces of
evil who want us all to die of bird
flu. That's why they want you to go
to the Eco Gardens.
```

'Whoever it is sounds deranged,' I say. 'How can anyone

take them seriously? It's really rude to call us "Freako-warrior".'

Evie looks thoughtful. 'Whoever it is seems to be obsessed by germs. Didn't Dad say that his colleague, George Whatsisname, is a hypochondriac? AND he works for the council, so he'd be bound to use their website. It could be him.'

'Maybe. But let's face it – it could be anyone.'

I stifle a yawn. I feel hot and tired. There is a sudden flash and, moments later, a loud crack of thunder.

'Global warming in action,' comments Evie. 'There are going to be a lot more storms as the earth heats up. Close the window, Lola – it's probably going to tip down with rain soon. We'd better switch off the computer before it blows up. Goodbye, stupid Whisperer.'

I shut the window quickly, looking out at the livid sky, which has cast a shroud of darkness over Frog Street.

'I hope the animals and birds at the Eco Gardens aren't too frightened,' I say. 'I'm not *too* worried – the keepers will make sure they're OK. Mr Macawber was so cool, wasn't he? When we go back, I want to ask if I can hold him.'

Evie's mum calls us down for supper – home-made fish pie and salad, no beans ... I remember Liam's remarks about beans and wind power, and I have to suppress a giggle. The supper is so delicious that I don't really care whether it's made from organic ingredients or not.

'I made the salad and the dressing,' says Evie's dad, proudly, as there is another flash of lightning, followed seconds later by a window-rattling clap of thunder which makes us all jump – storms make me nervous.

'I hope Wanda got home OK,' says Evie's mum, sounding worried.

'Oh, she probably made it home before the storm even started,' says Evie's dad, reassuringly.

'Do you think she *will* give the Eco Gardens a good write-up, Mum?' Evie asks.

'I'm sure she'll do her best, dear,' her mum replies.

Evie tells her parents about the Whisperer, and asks her dad if he thinks it could be his colleague on the council. But her dad laughs off the suggestion. 'George Pollard-Morris may be a bit of an old woman when it comes to germs,' he says, 'but he hasn't got a malicious bone in his body. I'm sure he would *never* spread nasty rumours. He would simply discuss his concerns at the next council meeting.'

After supper, Evie and I stack the dishwasher – a brand-new model with an energy-efficiency rating label of A++, Evie tells me proudly (I think Mum's clapped-out old machine has a rating of Z) – and make sure that it is on an economy setting. The thunder has rolled away into the distance and the rain is now pouring down outside.

'Just think how much water we'd save right now if we had a water butt,' says Evie, wiping the surfaces with Squirteco all-purpose cleaner. 'I persuaded Mum to switch to eco-friendly cleaning products.'

Evie seems to have parents who are a lot less resistant to going green than mine are! I can't help feeling jealous.

Liam arrives home soaking wet. After he has changed, he has his supper on a tray in front of the television and we all sit down to watch *Stars on Sunday*.

Evie and I are both yawning. Her mum suggests that we go and have relaxing showers.

'I wish we had a solar-power shower,' says Evie. 'Could we get one, Dad? Did you know that showering instead of bathing saves enough water each year to fill one hundred and thirty-two Olympic-size swimming pools?' (I think this was Eco-fact Number Twenty-three . . .)

'Well, you'll have to make do with an ordinary non-solar-power shower tonight,' says her mum.

'You go first,' Evie says to me. 'You're the guest. Enjoy your shower.'

'Make sure it's a cold one,' Liam calls after me. 'You don't want to use up all that energy on heating, do you? It's a hot night, after all.'

I flee upstairs, leaving Evie broaching the subject of water butts with her dad. She gets sent upstairs approximately thirty seconds later.

'I may have chosen the wrong moment,' she says. 'I'll try again tomorrow.'

I have my shower – I can't get the temperature right so it is a mixture of freezing and burning hot – and then I am worried about emerging from the bathroom wrapped in a towel, all pink and steamy like a lobster from my last burst of hot, in case Liam sees me: what if he comes upstairs at that exact moment? But Evie seems to have read my mind because she is just outside the bathroom door with a white fluffy bathrobe to tell me that the coast is clear.

She says that she has decided to clean out Posh and Pout's fish bowl instead of having a shower as she is tired. But she is not too tired, when she has finished cleaning out the fish, to whack me with a pillow, which starts our usual Eco-worriers' Night In Pillowfight. When we have had enough of whacking each other with pillows, we flop down on our beds, still laughing – Evie has made me a bed out of cushions, pillows and blankets on her bedroom floor.

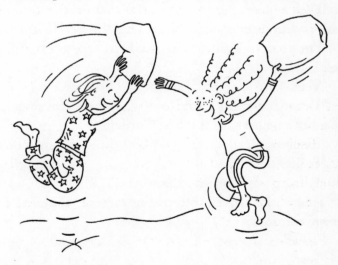

ECO-WORRIERS' PILLOWFIGHT

'It was really strange today,' I remark. 'I really enjoyed seeing all the birds and animals – especially Pablo. It was great to see him so happy and back with his friends. But it was sad seeing the Eco Gardens so empty. And why was Amelia there? She hates animals – she says they have fleas.'

'Penguins don't have fleas.'

'Amelia doesn't care – I just don't know what she was doing there.'

'She probably got dragged along by her parents,' Evie suggests. 'Although they looked out of place – especially her mum. And I didn't like the look of that Dean-boy who Liam knows.'

'Oh well,' I say, yawning. 'I think I'll just do a few stretches and then get some rest so that we can concentrate on important things like saving the Eco Gardens.'

'I'm tired, too,' says Evie. 'I didn't sleep last night . . . Lola?'

'Yes?'

'What if we can't find out who the Whisperer is? What if we can't save the Eco Gardens?'

'Evie?'

'Yes?'

'What if we can't save the world?'

Silence. I finish my stretching exercises and lie back on my cushions.

'Lola?'

'Yes?'

'Shall we finish those chocolate truffles?'

'Definitely! And throw me one of those back copies of *Green Teen* magazine. I feel like reading.'

Eco-fact Number Thirteen:

Increasing numbers of tourists are damaging fragile eco-systems by bringing litter and disease. A rat recently arrived on a cruise ship which brought visitors to the Galapagos Islands. It could have spread disease to native wild creatures.

I give an involuntary shiver. I wonder what kind of rat is spreading the evil rumours which could damage or even destroy the Eco Gardens?

Chapter Six

Four days have passed since our sleepover. Lying propped up by pillows on my bed, the window wide open to let in a cool early-morning breeze, I glance down at the diary open on my lap:

MONDAY
Evie and I sent a letter to The Shrubberylands Sentinel *to say what a great place the Eco Gardens is, and how all the animals and birds are well cared for. I hope they publish it.*

TUESDAY
*The Whisperer posted another nasty rumour on the council
website saying that a penguin has died of bird flu. We phone
Kate in a panic. She says that it is true that a penguin has
died, but it was of old age – nothing sinister. The Eco
Gardens' own website is denying all the rumours.*

WEDNESDAY
*The Whisperer is at it again! He or she said that soon all the
penguins at the Eco Gardens could be dropping like flies from
the deadly virus, which has already claimed one life. The
Whisperer goes on to say that the recent kidnapping of a penguin shows how security at the Eco Gardens is poor and so
the virus could easily spread into the community if another
penguin were to escape or be kidnapped.*

*I am FURIOUS!!! I got so worked up that Evie suggested
we let off steam by bouncing on the trampoline in her garden. Evie is very good at trampolining.*

THURSDAY
*In the afternoon Evie and I went swimming. Evie loves
diving, while I did lengths as part of my training for the
Olympics. Then we splashed each other. We kept thinking
everyone we saw was the Whisperer. This is not a good feeling. Mum and Dad came round to Evie's house this evening
for a drink and a chat. Dad drove me mad raving on about
what a great vehicle the Revro Widespace is – all he and
Evie's dad ever talk about is cars. BORING!*

Our parents don't seem at all bothered about saving either the planet or the Eco Gardens. Liam was more sympathetic and cheered Evie up by giving her an electric-guitar lesson – she sounded good and even Liam was impressed. Now I can't sleep because I am waiting for the morning to see if our letter has been published in The Shrubberylands Sentinel . . .

FRIDAY

So here I am, lying on my bed, chewing my pencil and waiting for Evie to arrive – she said that she would come straight round in the morning with the paper, as her parents get it delivered every Friday morning. My own parents hardly ever get newspapers or magazines, apart from Dad's favourite car magazine and Tent and Marquee News . . .

I hear someone open the front door, familiar footsteps thudding up the stairs, and Evie bursts into my room.

'Did they publish it?' I ask immediately – and then I see the look of dumbstruck horror on Evie's face. 'I'll take that as a "no", shall I?' I ask, as Evie flumps down on my bed and tosses the newspaper over to me.

'Not only is it not in there,' she says in a voice thick with anger and disappointment, 'but they've published a letter from someone who believes all the rumours and says that the Eco Gardens should be closed down immediately. But their pathetic Letters Page is nothing compared to . . . that!' She jabs at the front page with an angry finger.

I adjust my glasses as if I can hardly believe what I am seeing. It is awful.

A BREEDING GROUND FOR BIRD FLU?
screams the headline.

Underneath the headline are two photographs. One of them is of the Cuvier's Toucan, bathing in mud, and the other one appears to show a dead penguin covered in oil with litter strewn around it. I recognise it as being part of the display in the Education Zone to demonstrate the catastrophic effects on wildlife of oil spills and other pollution. But the photos are used in a deliberately misleading way, so that it looks as if they are showing appalling conditions at the Eco Gardens themselves. The article immediately below the photos reads:

The above photos which came into our possession suggest that birds are being kept in dreadful conditions at the local Ecological Gardens, which we understand is experiencing severe financial difficulties. It is alleged that a bird has recently died of the bird-flu virus. Should the Ecological Gardens be closed to the public immediately and should an exclusion zone be declared around it to prevent the spread of the deadly disease? Local Councillor, George Pollard-Morris, said, 'We have to take public health concerns seriously. Our environmental health inspectors will be carrying out a full inspection as a matter of urgency'.

It has also come to our attention that a penguin which escaped from the Eco Gardens was rescued and returned by two young girls. Is this further evidence that they don't look after their animals and birds?

'Oh! That is so WRONG!' I exclaim. 'Poor Kate! And why don't they talk to *us* so they can get their facts straight?'

'Because they're not interested in the truth,' says Evie, bitterly. 'They just want to make up a sensational story to scare people and sell their poxy paper. Come on, let's go back to my house right now – I want to talk to Mum and get her to talk to Wanda.'

'Who wrote the article, anyway?' I ask, my hands and my voice shaking with anger as we race back to Evie's house.

'The name of the reporter's at the top of the article. Look – it's someone called Rhona Tweeks. I don't know who she is, but she's a liar! Couldn't Wanda have stopped this from being published? Couldn't she have done *something*?' Evie is spluttering with rage, and I feel like crying.

We confront Evie's mum in the kitchen, spreading non-organic butter on her toast. 'Anything wrong, love?' she asks, looking up. 'Not a good headline, is it?' she says, looking at the front page of the *Sentinel* which Evie has just flung down on the kitchen table.

Evie opens and closes her mouth like a stranded fish. The she bursts into tears. This is too much for me, and I start crying, too.

'Mum! How could Wanda let this happen?'

'Oh, I'm sure it wasn't Wanda's fault,' says Evie's mum, looking worried and coming over to give each of us a hug. 'Please stop crying. I'm certain that Wanda wouldn't have had anything to do with this – she's the *Sentinel*'s sports reporter. She was very interested to hear about

Lola's Olympic hopes and dreams, and all your training,' Evie's mum adds, trying to cheer me up, but without much success.

'Can you ask Wanda to write an article saying how NOT true all these rumours are? And ask her to make sure *our* letter gets published? *Pleeease*, Mum?'

'I'll see what I can do,' Evie's mum replies. 'I have to go to work now. But I promise I'll talk to Wanda later. Cheer up, both of you!' She puts an arm around each of us. 'We know the rumours aren't true,' she says. 'I had a long chat with Kate when we visited the Eco Gardens because I was feeling a bit worried – but she told me that all their birds are regularly tested by the resident vet, and there is definitely no bird flu. So people will realise eventually that there's nothing to worry about.'

Evie smiles wanly. When her mum has gone, she turns to the Letters Page in the *Sentinel* and points to a letter headed *Virus Kills Penguin!* I read the letter, which I have not yet got round to looking at:

It is time that we all woke up to the fact that a local wildlife park – the Eco Gardens – could be harbouring a killer virus. I note that you have already had letters on this subject. One penguin has died already – how many more letters and how many more deaths will it take before the place is closed down and steps are taken to protect the public?
Yours faithfully,
Mr H Dean

'Who's Mr H Dean?' I ask, fuming. I feel as though I am going to explode with anger.

'I've no idea – except that he sounds like the Whisperer,' Evie replies, sitting down at her computer.

'What are you doing?'

'I'm going to Google Mr H Dean and Rhona Tweeks, in case we can find out anything about either of them.'

'It's really unlikely we'll find anything – and they may not even be using their real names,' I point out.

'I know, but I've got to try.'

There is nothing about Mr H Dean. Somehow this doesn't surprise me, although something about the name is bothering me.

'Look at this!' Evie exclaims. 'Rhona Tweeks is a well-known reporter – she's worked for all sorts of papers and magazines. And it says that she's married to David Plunkett of Plunkett's Plastics and has one daughter . . .'

'Amelia!' I shout.

'Yes!'

'So you mean that the woman we saw at the Eco Gardens with the blond hair and yellow mini-skirt, tottering around on ludicrously high heels – that was Rhona Tweeks? Also known as Mrs Plunkett?'

'Yes – I thought she looked fake!'

'So it was a disguise – so she could do her undercover reporting, knowing that no one would suspect someone who looked like a complete airhead?'

'Something like that. I expect she had a camera with

her, so she could have taken these photos.' Evie points to the photos of the toucan and apparently-dead penguin on the front page.

'But why would she do it?' I ask, frowning and chewing my bottom lip.

'I don't know, but I'm going to Google David Plunkett,' says Evie. 'There's something about all the Plunketts that I just don't like!'

Evie finds information about David Plunkett's meteoric rise in the world of business to become founder and owner of the hugely successful Plunkett's Plastics Company.

'It says here that he has "plans for expansion"' Evie says.

'He was quite fat,' I say, jokingly. 'His waistline probably has plans for expansion!'

'Ha ha! But it's more likely to mean that he wants to build more stores to sell his horrible plastic stuff.'

Evie clicks on to the Eco Gardens website, on the home page of which is the following announcement:

```
We would like you to know that there
is not a word of truth in the article
on the front page of today's edition
of The Shrubberylands Sentinel. We
have launched a formal objection and
the newspaper has agreed to print an
apology in the next edition for any
wrong impression it may have given.
```

> The Gardens will be closed on Monday
> while an environmental health inspec-
> tion takes place. We are confident
> that the results will allay any
> remaining fears that any of you may
> have. We would like to thank our loyal
> friends and visitors for their mes-
> sages of support.

'That's good,' I say. 'It sounds like there are other people out there who know the rumours aren't true.'

Outside the window, the clouds have gone and it is a fine, sunny day. I begin to feel more cheerful.

'Kate needs all the support she can get,' says Evie. 'Let's go to the Eco Gardens now and see if there's anything we can do to help. She told me after our last visit that, as Pablo's rescuers, we're welcome any time – although Mum said we mustn't keep bothering her.'

'I'm sure she won't mind if we just go there today, and I don't want to sit around doing nothing – I want to do *something*,' I say.

Evie changes into her favourite blue organic T-shirt with the dolphin motif – she also has a white one with a penguin motif, but it is in the wash – and her brown cropped trousers, and goes to the bathroom to tame her curls with some water.

'There!' she says, sticking a green star on her eco-chart. 'I get a star for dressing in organic clothes. Is that skirt organic?'

'No, it came from the same shop where I saw that really cool red and orange top with the smiley face on it, only you wouldn't let me get it because —'

'It was probably produced in a sweatshop by a child labourer, working in dreadful slum conditions for next-to-nothing, so that people here can wear cheap, fashionable clothes. Would you want that on your conscience?'

'Er, no,' I reply, sighing. It was *such* a cool red and orange top . . .

'Come on,' exclaims Evie. 'Let's get going. It's a long walk.'

'I don't mind,' I say. 'It's not *that* far, and walking is good exercise and more eco-friendly than going there in a gas-guzzling 4x4. It can count as part of my training for the Olympics!'

Halfway there, I'm feeling very hot. Evie has stopped chatting and is getting to get out of breath. We're walking along a track beside the main road. A sign tells us that we have three kilometres left until we reach the Eco Gardens.

'It didn't seem so far in the 4x4,' I comment.

'Be quiet a moment,' says Evie. 'Listen!'

I listen. In the distance I can hear a faint but familiar sound – the discordant jingle of Meltonio's ice-cream van. It is the tune of 'Oh I Do Like to be Beside the Seaside!' at varying speeds. Soon we see him driving slowly along the road towards us, a queue of cars following him and attempting to overtake him whenever there is a gap in the traffic coming the other way.

He draws up alongside us, the jingle slowing right down and sounding very sick.

'Want a lift?' he asks.

'Yes, please!' we both say, quickly. There is room for two passengers on the front seat alongside Meltonio.

'Put on your seatbelts, please,' he says. 'Let's go!'

It is a strange feeling gliding along in such a quiet

82

vehicle – apart from the jingle playing through a speaker on the roof above our heads. I have never been for a ride in an ice-cream van before. Evie looks pleased, too – she can't stop smiling.

Meltonio expresses his outrage at this morning's newspaper article. 'But we will not let these bad people, whoever they are, stop our wonderful Eco Gardens, will we?' he roars suddenly, making us both jump.

'No!' we agree, vehemently. Then we all sing along to the jingle playing over our heads. Meltonio seems to enjoy singing 'Oh I Do Like to be Beside the Seaside!' in a rich operatic baritone voice, although I can't help thinking he must get sick of hearing that same tune, day after day . . . especially at the wrong speed.

Kate seems downcast. There have been so few visitors that she has decided to close for the day.

'But the paper's going to print a full apology,' Evie exclaims.

'AND you'll be cleared by that health check on Monday,' I add, encouragingly. 'Then business will pick up again – you'll see.'

Meltonio nods agreement, and hands us all ice-creams.

Kate sighs. 'So much damage has been done by the rumours, even when they're proved not to be true. Mud sticks – just like it does to our toucan when it's taking a mud bath. The council may not renew my lease, and even if they do, we might have to close.'

Evie and I gasp in horror. 'No!' we exclaim.

'It costs loads of money every day to look after our animals,' Kate explains. 'We rely on visitor numbers, grants and charitable donations, and some of our donors have already withdrawn their support. I may not have a choice.' Kate looks even sadder.

'We'll raise money,' Evie says. 'We'll organise events ... How about a concert to raise money and awareness? We could invite Dodo to sing at it.'

'Thanks,' says Kate, forcing a smile. 'But stars like Dodo get booked up months, even years, in advance, and I could never afford her fee.'

Evie looks disappointed. Then she cheers up. 'I know. I'll get my brother and his band to perform for nothing – I'm sure they'd do it. And I'll make a petition to save the Eco Gardens – I know plenty of people who'd sign it.'

'You're very kind,' says Kate. 'I know you want to help. There *is* something you could do. We're printing out flyers at the moment in my office. My team and I thought we'd hand them out to the public to deny the rumours and invite people to come along after next Monday and see the Gardens and claim a free drink in the Eco-Café. Would you like to help hand them out?'

'Oh, yes!' we chorus.

'I'll get some paper for the petition, too,' Kate says as she rushes off.

While we are waiting, Evie and I go to see the penguins. The Eco Gardens look beautiful and the sunlight dances on the surface of the penguin pool.

Several penguins slide on their bellies – plop! – into the water and come speeding towards us under the surface – little dark shapes, like mini torpedoes, which suddenly shoot up out of the water and land on their feet on the pebbly beach nearest to us.

'Pablo!' I exclaim.

Meltonio wanders over to join us.

'Hello, Pablo,' he says. 'He is a splendid fellow! But I must go into town and sell some ices there. I need to earn money.'

'We'll come with you,' Evie says. 'That would be the best place to hand out the flyers – right in the middle of town where there are lots of people.'

Kate walks towards us, and hands me a box full of flyers, printed on recycled paper. Mr Macawber is sitting on her shoulder.

'Can I hold him?' Evie asks.

'Yes, sure. He might scratch your bare skin with his feet though,' Kate says, and gives Evie a special arm guard to wear before carefully transferring the macaw on to her outstretched arm.

Evie giggles. 'I can feel him holding on!' she exclaims.

'He seems a bit off-colour today,' says Kate. 'Not quite his normal self. I hope he's not sickening for something. Don't worry – there's no chance it's bird flu,' she adds, hastily. 'All our birds are regularly tested by the vet.'

Mr Macawber puts his head on one side and looks at

Evie out of his yellow-ringed eye. Evie puts her head on one side and looks back at him. He seems sad and ruffled today and his feathers look dull.

Kate sighs. 'I don't know why, but this morning, for no reason at all, he suddenly said, "Stupid parrot"! I've certainly *never* taught him to say that,' she says. 'And now he won't say anything. I'm going to have him checked over by the vet.'

Meltonio signs the petition with a flourish, and then we set off in the ice-cream van for Shrubberylands. As we pull up in the parking area at one side of the Shopping Zone, we see Amelia Plunkett approaching with her best friend, Jemima Trilling.

'Duck down!' Evie whispers to me. Although riding in Meltonio's van is great fun as well as being eco-friendly, it is not the coolest form of transport, despite all the ices, and Amelia likes to find any reason for making fun of us. Not that we care, of course, but we could do without it.

Too late. We have been spotted.

'Oh!' exclaims Amelia, staring in through the open window. 'You two *really* like ice-cream, don't you? What sort of clothes do you call those?' she adds, pointing rudely at Evie's outfit. Evie looks great in her blue dolphin top and cropped trousers – she is definitely more hip than hippy!

'Eco-chic,' Evie snaps back. 'My mum sells it at her shop, and it's the best.'

AMELIA AND JESSICA

'Freako-chic, more like!' Amelia jokes, and Jemima giggles – she has a very annoying high-pitched giggle.

They move away to buy Organic Death by Chocolate Triple Flakes from Meltonio, who is already busy selling his ices in the back of the van.

'Lola,' Evie hisses at me, 'I think it's her.'

'Who? What are you talking about?'

'Amelia – she's the Whisperer! She just used the word "freako-chic" – and on the website she called us "freako-warriors". And she's Plunkett's daughter.'

'Mmm,' I ponder. 'I wonder if you're right . . .'

We mingle with the crowd of shoppers, handing out

flyers from the box. Only a few people refuse to take one. Evie also persuades several people to sign the petition.

'Look, there are the Three Witches,' I say, nudging Evie's arm.

Mrs Fossett, Mrs Baggot and Mrs Throgmorton have just emerged from the Easybuy Bargainstore, carrying loads of plastic bags.

> ### Eco-fact Number Nineteen:
> Globally, between five hundred billion and one trillion plastic bags are produced annually. It takes one hundred years for a plastic bag to rot down.

'And I bet they don't re-use those bags, the wasteful old bats!' Evie exclaims. 'We should be like Tanzania in Africa and ban all plastic bags.'

'Uh-oh – they've seen us.'

Mrs Fossett is holding up a copy of the *The Shrubberylands Sentinel* with its stupid headline and photos, and she is smirking at us. Mrs Baggot and Mrs Throgmorton smirk, too.

'They're so mean,' Evie fumes.

We decide that we won't bother giving them a flyer and nearly all the flyers have gone anyway, so we visit Evie's mum in her shop and tell her about our day. She says that she will give us a lift home, so we go to say goodbye to Meltonio, who is doing good business. He assures us that he will be back at the Eco Gardens later in the week.

Evie and I feel pleased that we have achieved something today in handing out the flyers, but we are still very, VERY worried.

Chapter Seven

Eco-fact Number Fourteen:
A holiday flight to the Canaries produces a tonne of carbon, equivalent to an average household's entire electricity output for a whole year.

Things to Worry About:

1) The Parent Plunketts
2) The Plunkett offspring aka Amelia aka The Whisperer (we think)
3) The letter-writer (who *is* Mr H Dean?)
4) Mr Macawber. But now I think perhaps Mr Macawber should be at the top of the list, and I am worried because I don't know which I should be more worried about . . .
5) A huge spot above my left eyebrow.

'I can't even see a spot,' I say, putting down Evie's latest list and peering at the area just above her left eyebrow.

'It's probably hiding among the freckles,' Evie replies. 'But I can *feel* it.'

We have recently returned from the Shopping Zone with Evie's mum in the Roadhog Runabout – but we were grateful for the lift, emissions or no emissions, although Evie had to stick a black footprint on her eco-chart to ease her conscience. Evie has sent an email to Kate to tell her that we successfully handed out the flyers, and to ask how Mr Macawber is. As yet there is no reply.

'I *do* hope he's all right,' I say, trying not to imagine Mr Macawber lying on his back with his feet in the air.

'Your dad's just got home,' I say, looking out of the window as I often do – I am always on the lookout for rare or unusual birds.

'Great,' replies Evie, 'let's go and ask him if he knows anything about the Plunketts and the lease on the Eco Gardens.

We rush out of Evie's room and nearly collide with Liam, who is crossing the landing.

'Whoa!' he calls out. 'What's the big hurry? I thought you two were into conserving energy, like I am.'

'And how exactly do you conserve energy, Liam?' Evie asks.

'By lying down, mostly,' he replies.

'Of course,' says Evie. 'Silly me.'

We find Evie's dad in the kitchen, making himself a mug of Fair Trade tea.

DAVID PLUNKETT AND MRS PLUNKETT

'What do you know about David Plunkett, Dad?' Evie demands.

'That's an unusual question to be asked the moment I get home,' says her dad. 'I suppose it makes a change from asking when I'm going to lag the loft!'

'Dad, seriously. It's important.'

Evie's dad sighs. 'It's funny that you should mention David Plunkett,' he says. 'He's just made an offer to buy the land which the Eco Gardens is on for a very large amount of money, on condition that he is given planning permission for a retail park.'

Evie and I look at each other open-mouthed.

'But ... but ... Dad! The council won't accept Plunkett's offer, will they?' Evie stammers. 'It would mean the end of the Eco Gardens!'

'I know, love,' says Evie's dad wearily, stirring two tea-spoons of sugar into his tea. 'Unfortunately, not everyone feels as strongly about wildlife as you do. Many on the council feel that they should accept this offer – they could do with the money, and there have been a lot of problems at the wildlife park recently.'

'We must do something!' Evie protests. 'If we get a petition to keep the Eco Gardens open, will the council change its mind?'

'It would certainly listen to the viewpoint of local residents,' her dad replies.

'Good! Because I've already started a petition, and loads of people are going to sign it!'

'We could take it round the houses of everyone we know from school,' I suggest.

'You could also ask Mr Patel if he'd display it on the counter in the local shop,' Evie's dad suggests. 'And people could sign it when they go to pay for their shopping.'

'Great idea, Dad. Thanks.'

Liam has come into the kitchen to raid the fridge. Evie asks him if he and his band would play at a concert to save the Eco Gardens. Liam says that he will think about it, but the answer is probably yes. Evie gives him a hug.

'Help!' exclaims Liam. 'Seriously worrying sisterly behaviour! Help!'

I wish I was brave enough to give Liam a hug. Liam has finished raiding the fridge, and has now turned his attention to the biscuit tin. 'I heard you talking about David Plunkett,' he says. 'I was chatting with some mates the other day and said that I'd seen Dean Hughes at the

Eco Gardens. They told me that he's working at the Plunkett's Plastics store.'

Evie looks at me. I look at Evie.

'Mr H Dean!' we both exclaim.

'Who? What?' Liam looks confused.

'The person who wrote that letter to the *Sentinel* spreading nasty rumours about the Eco Gardens – he signed himself as Mr H Dean,' I explain. 'It's Dean Hughes, only the other way round! It's him!'

'It's an evil Plunkett plot. Plunkett's causing all the problems at the Eco Gardens because he wants to get them closed down so that he can buy up the land and build there!' I exclaim. Finally it all makes sense.

'Lola's right. Dean Hughes is obviously helping David Plunkett with his dirty work,' says Evie. 'I expect he's doing it for money.'

'That sounds like Dean,' Liam agrees.

Evie and I can't stop talking about the evil Plunkett who is causing all the problems at the Eco Gardens. We are horrified that he got his wife to write the damaging article published in the paper, and even his daughter is part of the plot, posting nasty messages on the council website.

Evie's dad looks thoughtful, and then interrupts us. 'I think you should remember that you don't have any positive proof of any of this,' he says. 'So be careful what you accuse people of.'

'OK, Dad.'

Liam follows us out of the kitchen and, when we are

out of earshot of Dad, he suggests that we visit Plunkett's store soon and see if we can pick up any clues. Evie wants to go immediately, but Liam points out that it will be closing by the time we get there. He suggests that we go another day, and says that he will come with us as he doesn't want us getting into any sort of trouble. He suggests we go on Tuesday, which would fit in OK with his band practice, and other things.

'You're really lucky to have a brother like Liam,' I say, as we go back to Evie's room.

Evie looks surprised, as if this is a new and unusual thought. 'I suppose you're right,' she says.

'Do you think there's a reply from Kate yet?' I ask, as Evie sits down at the computer.

'I'll check.'

There is an email from Kate. Evie reads it to me as my eyes are getting tired.

Had a shock just after you left today. Mr Macawber keeled right over - I thought he was dead! But the vet ran tests and said that he'd been given a small amount of poison, but luckily he's a very strong parrot and he survived - against the odds. Don't know how on earth this could have happened . . . Someone is out to get us . . . But what kind of sick individual attacks the animals themselves? I

am really worried. Perhaps I had better give up the Eco Gardens so the
animals can go to other zoos and be
safe. But the thought breaks my heart.
Mr Macawber had a long sleep but he's
coming round now, though still rather
woozy and unsteady on his feet. The
vet says he'll recover. The police
have taken footage from the parrotcam
to examine. Environmental inspection
on Monday. Ask your journalist friend
to come along so they can be first to
see everything is fine. You can come
too, if allowed. Let me know.

Kate

SICK PARROT

'Oh, thank goodness! Mr Macawber's OK!' I exclaim. I hug Evie, and she hugs me back. 'Evie, do you think Dean gave him the poison? Or maybe it was someone else who Plunkett bribed to do his dirty work?'

Evie runs her hands through her curls in a gesture of disbelief and exasperation. 'Who knows what any of them are capable of?'

There is a knock on the door and Evie's mum comes into the room. 'I've just arrived back with Wanda,' she says. 'We met in town for a chat, and she's come here to assure you that she had nothing to do with that article.'

Wanda steps into the room. 'OK if I come in?' she asks.

'Oh, yes,' we both say. If Wanda had nothing to do with the bad article, perhaps she can help to put things right. We tell Mum and Wanda everything, including our very strong suspicion that the Whisperer is Amelia Plunkett and the letter-writer is someone who works for Plunkett. We ask Wanda if she'll accept Kate's invitation to come along to the Eco Gardens on Monday to see for herself that everything's fine.

'Then you can write an article saying that all these rumours are rubbish and Amelia Plunkett is an idiot and so is Dean Hughes!' Evie exclaims. 'And Rhona Tweeks is Mrs Plunkett – and now we know why she's telling lies and spreading nasty rumours: to help her husband with his horrible expansion plans!'

Wanda laughs nervously. Then, seeing our pleading expressions, she says, 'Look, I'll make a quick phone call and clear it with my editor. I'm certainly willing to come along to the Eco Gardens on Monday and find out the facts and set the record straight, once and for all. But I won't name names. Rhona Tweeks is a friend of the editor and I don't think we had any reason to suspect her at the time – although it's fair to say we're unlikely to publish any of her articles ever again. Hang on, I'll phone my editor now.'

Wanda makes a call on her mobile to check with her editor, and after ten minutes she gives us the thumbs-up sign. 'Well, that's settled, then,' she says, beaming at us. 'It'll make a change from covering the local hockey-league matches!'

We ask if we can come along as well, explaining that Kate said that we could come too if we were allowed. Evie's mum says yes, and Wanda tells us that she will pick us up at nine on Monday morning. Before she leaves, she signs Evie's petition. Evie's mum says that I can stay again on Sunday night so that Evie and I are both ready to go on Monday morning.

When Evie's mum and Wanda have gone, we decide to design a poster on the computer to reinforce what the flyers said about the rumours being untrue and that people are welcome to visit the Eco Gardens after next Monday and claim their free drink in the café. Evie decorates the border of the poster with a penguin design, and we print out several dozen.

'We can hand these to people when we go collecting signatures for the petition,' says Evie, 'and ask them to put them up in their windows.'

'Let's go now!' I say, enthusiastically. 'We could go through the park – I feel in need of a jog.' I don't want my training schedule to slip.

On the way to the park, we pass Mum clipping our hedge. I am disappointed – I wanted her to let it grow, just to annoy Mrs Fossett, and also because an overgrown hedge encourages birds and other wildlife to hide in it.

'Hello, love,' she says, putting down her clippers. I suppose I should be pleased that she is not using an electric hedge trimmer. 'Phew! Isn't it hot?' she says, wiping her brow.

'It's the effect of global warming, Mum. That's why we need to get a wind turbine put on the roof, so that we can reduce our carbon footprint. I hope you remembered to get those low-energy light bulbs.'

'I'm sorry, love – it's too hot to worry about global warming,' Mum says with a sigh.

I despair.

I decide to go into the house to change into my running gear – shorts, T-shirt, trainers – leaving Evie to tell Mum about the evil Plunkett plot and get her to sign the petition and take a poster.

'We're just off to the park, Mum – OK? Love you!' I blow her a kiss and set off down the road at a steady jog, with Evie complaining just behind me.

'I'm nearly dropping these posters – couldn't you slow down?'

'No! We need to hurry if we're going to save the Eco

Gardens – and the world!' I call back over my shoulder, just before I trip over Boris the cat.

'Are you OK, Lola?' Evie asks anxiously, as I pull myself back to my feet from the grass verge where I landed. Fortunately I avoided landing heavily on the hard pavement.

'I'm fine. I think I've got a bruise on my knee, but that's all. Now you know why they don't allow cats at the Olympics.'

I love jogging around the park – it has recently become one of my favourite things to do. So I don't appreciate being laughed and jeered at by Amelia and Jemima, who are sitting side by side on the little low swings in the kiddies' play area. A small child is standing nearby, unable to use the swings because Amelia and Jemima's backsides are occupying them.

I think I hear Evie snarl at the sight of them, although I may be mistaken about this. But she certainly doesn't look very pleased to see them, and she advances towards them in a menacing un-Evie-like manner with me just a few paces behind. Jemima looks worried. But Amelia stifles a yawn, and says, 'Hello, sad freakoes!'

'Hello, Amelia,' hisses Evie in a strange, harsh whisper, bending down quite close to Amelia's face so that she can hear.

Amelia looks startled. 'Er, I know you're weird,' she says, 'but why are you whispering?'

'You should know,' hisses Evie in the same harsh whisper.

I can't help grinning – Amelia looks as if a large lump has lodged in her throat and she can't swallow it.

'Don't think you've won – the battle isn't over *yet*,' hisses Evie. I have never seen her so fierce! Her green eyes flash and her wild red curls make her look like Boudicca, fiery Celtic queen of the ancient Britons. All she needs is for her face to be covered in blue woad.

We walk away, leaving Amelia and Jemima both looking like rabbits caught in headlights.

Soon Evie and I are laughing so much that we have to stop to catch our breath. Before we leave the park, we attach one of the posters to a tree with drawing pins which Evie thoughtfully brought along.

We go to as many of our friends' houses as we can, and collect a lot of signatures on our petition. Nearly everyone takes a poster, apart from one family who seem to be very worried by the whole thing, and look at us as though *we* might be carrying the bird-flu virus. This is upsetting, but Mr Patel cheers us up by agreeing to display the petition on the counter of his shop, for people to sign. We agree to collect it at the end of the week. Evie buys some chocolate – it is the sugar rush hour!

On our way back through the park we find that our poster has been torn down, crumpled and thrown on the ground. Picking it up, I see that someone has written *Come and see the dead penguins!* on it in an untidy scrawl, using what looks like lipstick to write with.

'Amelia's pathetic revenge,' Evie comments.

'She's so stupid,' I agree. 'Why can't she see that animals and birds are more important than her dad's horrible plastic stuff?'

'Because she's an airhead and all she can think about is the next shopping expedition and how much money her dad's going to lavish on her.'

'Do you think there's any chance that one day she'll realise that there are more important things than shopping?' I ask. I enjoy shopping but, unlike Amelia, I don't think I could devote my life to it.

'No chance! Well, you never know. But I think it's unlikely. She told me at school that she likes global warming because it means that she'll get to wear her bikini and get a tan for more of the year!'

We walk home through the park in silence. It is very peaceful: ducks are drifting around on the pond, and people are sitting on benches or walking their dogs.

I decide to go home for a shower. Evie says that she will text me later.

I feel tired, but pleased that our petition is going well. I can't wait to tell Kate about it on Monday.

Late in the evening I get a text from Evie. *Gr8 news!* it says. *The spot over my left eyebrow has completely disappeared.*

Eco-fact Number Seventy-two:

Devon's highways department says that street lighting is responsible for nearly forty per cent of the county council's carbon footprint. Devon could become England's darkest county if plans to turn off street lights to save energy are approved.

Chapter Eight

Early on Monday morning, Evie and I are ready and waiting outside Evie's house when Wanda pulls up in a red Citroën C3 Stop and Start. Wanda explains that it disengages the engine automatically when the car is stationary in order to save fuel – a really good idea! There is a photographer from *The Shrubberylands Sentinel*, a young man dressed in black, in the front passenger seat, so Evie and I get in the back. Mrs Fossett has been watching us suspiciously over the top of her immaculately-trimmed privet hedge. I get the impression she thinks we should be served with an Anti-social Behaviour Order, just for hanging around outside our house!

As we approach the Eco Gardens' car park, we pass a police car, which is just leaving. Kate is standing near one of the entrance booths, and greets us warmly. She looks tired and pale.

'We've had a disturbed night,' she explains. 'The Howler Monkeys sounded the alarm in the early hours of the morning. Someone had been in and had tried to cut a hole in the fence round Chris the South American Rhea's enclosure, but they must have panicked when they heard the Howler Monkeys, and they dropped their wire cutters and ran. So the police have taken the wire cutters for examination.'

Evie and I exchange looks. But before we can say anything, Kate has to go and welcome the two Environmental Inspectors who have just arrived with Evie's dad's colleague, George Pollard-Morris. They look serious but not unfriendly, and Kate seems confident that they are not going to find anything amiss.

While the inspection is taking place, Kate suggests that Evie and I go to Encounter Village where Mr Macawber is recuperating. She and Wanda and the photographer are going to accompany the inspectors and George Pollard-Morris.

'The police and I have been looking at the parrotcam footage,' she says. 'We saw a youth who seemed to be talking to Mr Macawber for a long time, then he reached out his hand towards the macaw and appeared to feed him something, which is strictly against the rules, of course. There are signs everywhere saying that members of the public must NOT feed the animals, because they might make them ill. So the police think the youth must have slipped poor Mr Macawber the poison, but they haven't been able to identify him yet. I've seen him here quite often in recent weeks but I thought he was just interested in the animals and birds – I didn't realise he was up to anything bad.'

'Did he look like a rat?' Evie blurts out.

Kate looks surprised. 'Well, er, slightly, I suppose. Why? Do you know him?'

'Liam knows who he is – his name's Dean Hughes and he was always getting into trouble at school,' Evie says in a rush.

'Oh, that's very helpful information!' Kate exclaims. 'I'll pass those details on to the police – they'll probably want to have a word with you and Liam at some point – but thanks. I'd better go now and join the Environmental Inspectors.' Kate hurries away.

The Eco Gardens, baking under an already-hot sun, seem eerie and empty without visitors. The refreshment kiosk is boarded up and the flowers in the borders seem to be wilting in the heat. We pass one of the keepers repairing the damage to Chris the Rhea's enclosure. The gibbons are going 'WOOH! WOOH!' nearby.

'At least the animals are happy,' Evie remarks.

'They certainly are,' I agree, as we pass a cage full of Laughing Kookaburras on our way into Encounter Village. On one side is a pen containing a pair of Vietnamese Pot-Bellied Pigs, and a couple of large enclosures containing Monty the Royal Python, Vinnie the Vine Snake and Colin the Corn Snake. On the other side is a grassy area inside a low wire fence where big lop-eared rabbits are grazing and chickens with huge feathery feet strut around, going '*Boc boc boc*'.

We ask a keeper where Mr Macawber is, and he points to a cage in the corner.

'Hi, Mr Macawber,' I say, gently. Mr Macawber appears to be asleep on his perch. He still looks ruffled. But then he opens one eye and tilts his head to look at us.

'Hello!' says Evie. 'Are you feeling better?

'Who did this to you?' I ask, leaning towards Mr Macawber. 'Was it Dean Hughes?'

'I wish he could tell us,' says Evie.

Mr Macawber shuffles along his perch, first one way, then the other.

'Stupid parrot,' he says suddenly in his strangled voice.

Evie jumps. Although Kate told us that Mr Macawber has starting saying 'Stupid parrot' it sounds strange to hear him actually say it.

'You're *not* stupid!' I exclaim. '*Clever* parrot!'

Mr Macawber does some more shuffling.

We both stand staring at the macaw, waiting for him to say it again. But Mr Macawber says nothing more. He appears to have gone back to sleep.

'You'd better leave him to have a rest,' says the keeper, coming up to us. 'He's still recovering.'

'OK,' says Evie. 'But have you heard him saying anything?'

'Yes, he keeps saying "Stupid parrot". No one knows why.'

'The boy who gave him the poison probably taught him to say it,' I suggest.

The keeper looks upset – he obviously feels personally responsible for someone managing to poison Mr Macawber.

'But he's definitely on the mend,' I say brightly, trying to cheer the keeper up.

Evie and I leave Encounter Village and walk towards Penguin Paradise. The Environmental Inspectors are walking round the penguin pool, followed closely by Kate and Wanda.

'Very well cared-for animals and birds – and happy penguins!' remarks one of inspectors, nodding approvingly. 'Very good indeed!'

Kate grins and gives us the thumbs-up. Wanda is scribbling away in her notebook. The photographer snaps away, taking penguin photos. Annie the Penguin Keeper arrives with the penguins' next meal – fish and no chips. She manages to single out Pablo from the rest of the crowd so that the photographer can get a good shot of him. After that, he takes a photo of Evie and me.

'Where's Mr Pollard-Morris?' I ask.

'Oh, he got too close to the Howler Monkeys and they howled at him so loudly that he went quite white, poor man! So we sent him to the Eco-Café for a nice cup of Fair Trade tea.'

Evie tells Kate about the petition and that she has

FISH AND NO CHIPS!

already gathered plenty of signatures and Kate is very pleased.

I decide to do some bird-watching. It is fun watching Chris the Rhea through my binoculars. Then I decide to look at the birds I noticed flying near the woodland area. Evie wanders along behind me – she is not quite so interested in birds.

So she must think that I have gone completely mad when I suddenly shout 'YESSS!!!' and start running round in circles and doing star-jumps because I have just spotted a GOLDEN ORIOLE!!!

'Oof! I'm . . . er . . . glad you're so pleased, Lola, but could you stop hugging me now? I . . . can't . . . breathe!'

'Sorry,' I say, releasing Evie. I explain why I am so

excited, and manage to point out another Golden Oriole to Evie, who tries to look interested. 'It's really unusual to see one – I'm so lucky! Let's go closer to the trees – it'd be great if I could get a photo on my phone.'

The woodland floor is soft and springy and twigs snap under our feet. It is cooler among the trees, and smells of crushed green leaves.

'We'd better be quiet,' I whisper, 'so that we don't scare them away.' I am holding my binoculars to my eyes and have my camera phone in the other hand. 'Oh, wow!' I exclaim, softly.

'What is it?' whispers Evie.

'They've got a nest! Look – up in that tree . . . See?' I gaze upwards.

'Oh, yes! There it is.'

'And there's the male, just flying up to the nest with a grub in his beak. I know it's the male because of its bright yellow body and black wings. It's amazing that they're actually nesting in this country – it used to be too cold for them. They're incredibly rare . . .'

I manage to get some photos. Evie soon gets bored of Golden Orioles, so we go to the Eco-Café for a drink. It is only serving Fair Trade coffee and tea and a few snacks laid on especially for the Environmental Inspectors, so we get two bottles of water out of the vending machine. George Pollard-Morris is still sitting in a corner, stirring his tea. I get the impression that he is not all that keen on animals, but he agrees to sign Evie's petition when she approaches him. She has brought a spare sheet which she

can attach to the rest of the petition when we get it back from Mr Patel's shop.

Kate seems much happier when it is time for us to leave – the Health and Safety Inspection has gone really well. She says that she has been thinking about Evie's suggestion that there should be a concert to raise money and awareness, and she now thinks that we should go ahead and organise it.

'I think it should be a Family Fun Day and Concert in aid of the Eco Gardens,' she says. I ask if we could call it the 'Pablo Appeal' in aid of the Eco Gardens and penguins in their natural habitat. Kate thinks this is a good idea for raising public awareness, and we can use Pablo as a symbol of hope.

'Would you mention the Fun Day at the end of your

article?' she asks Wanda. 'Shall I plan it for Saturday in – oh, say three weeks' time? Yes, that would do nicely! Gates open at ten in the morning – free fun packs for the under-tens!'

'Er, sure,' says Wanda, smiling nervously. 'I'll give it a mention. But isn't there rather a lot to organise? Are you going to do it all in time?'

'I will,' Kate replies. 'I'm not sleeping much at the moment – I think it's because of all the worry. It will do me good to have something to focus on. And the situation is urgent!'

It is good to see Kate regaining her energy and enthusiasm. I tell her about the Golden Oriole, and she says that she is pleased that it is nesting in the woodland, but she seems distracted by thoughts about the Fun Day, and is hardly listening.

Wanda says that she has more than enough material for her article – the photographer has gone to the Eco-Café for a cup of coffee – and that she will now take us home. We tell Kate that we're willing to talk to the police about Dean Hughes, but she replies that their inquiries take a while and that, unfortunately, a poisoned parrot is not at the top of their list of Worst Crimes.

'But it should be!' Evie protests.

Kate assures us that, if she sees that it *is* the same boy as on the parrotcam, she will pass on the information we gave her to the police, and says that we are bound to hear from them in due course. In the meantime, she will personally make sure that Dean Hughes isn't allowed anywhere near the Eco Gardens.

Evie and I are happy to go home now. Evie wants to tell Liam that the concert is definitely *on*, and I can't wait to tell EVERYONE about the Golden Oriole.

With so much going on, we hardly have time to worry!

Eco-fact Number Nine:

Polar bears today are thinner and less healthy than those of twenty years ago because the ice breaks up two weeks earlier in spring, robbing them of two weeks' hunting.

Chapter Nine

Evie and I have discovered that Wanda is also a big fan of Dodo, and she tells us that she once met Dodo at the end of a concert and got her autograph. Wanda says that Dodo was really nice and that she has a kind heart – she owns two dogs which she got from a rescue centre when no one else wanted them because one of them was blind in one eye and the other one was deaf. We belt out a few of her best ballads in the car going home, with all the windows open and the breeze blowing our hair in all directions. I am not sure that the photographer is such a big fan of Dodo – he looks *very* relieved when we turn into Frog Street.

'Whose car is that?' asks Evie, parting a thick curtain of tangled curls which have fallen across her face. 'Look – on our drive. I don't recognise it.'

'It's a Monda Civic Hybrid,' says Wanda, who seems to know a thing or two about cars. 'It runs partly on petrol and partly on a rechargeable battery, so it's more energy efficient.'

We get out of Wanda's car and have a closer look at the car on the drive. It is green in colour, and very shiny and new.

'Do you like it?' asks Evie's dad, coming out of the house with a broad smile on his face.

'Dad!' exclaims Evie. 'You're home early.'

'I had to go and pick up our new car,' says her dad.

'Our new car?' Evie looks at her dad in wonder. 'Where . . . where's the 4x4?' she asks.

'I traded it in – for this!' Evie's dad pats the new car affectionately on the roof. 'I call it the Clean Green Eco-friendly Machine. Are you pleased?'

'Oh, Dad! Of course I'm pleased!' Evie gives him a big hug. 'I like it loads better than the 4x4. It's really cool – and so are you!'

I can't help feeling a twinge of jealousy – Evie's parents are so much more eco-aware than mine.

Evie's dad grins, and invites everyone in for a cup of tea and a slice of the date-and-walnut loaf which he made at the weekend.

'I'll be able to grow my own dates soon,' he says, 'if the weather goes on getting hotter.'

I notice out of the kitchen window that clouds are building up in the sky over the roofs of Frog Street. I wonder if there is going to be another storm . . .

Evie tells her dad about the day's events. He promises to support the Fun Day in any way he can, and says that he will have to give it some thought. Almost immediately he has one helpful idea – he says that Kate will have to apply to the council for a licence to stage a concert, but he promises to get her application processed quickly.

'Thanks, Dad – Kate will be really pleased.'

I am looking at the photos of the Golden Oriole on my phone, and I can't help smiling as I tell Evie's dad about the exciting moment when I spotted it. 'It's an endangered species that's hardly ever been seen in this country before, and it's actually nesting in the woodlands at the Eco Gardens —'

'That is INCREDIBLE!' exclaims Evie's dad, so loudly that we all jump, and Wanda spills her tea.

Evie's dad thumps the table. 'Do you realise what you've done?' he asks me.

'Er . . . no . . .' I am feeling rather scared, and wish I'd kept quiet like I normally do. I seem to have driven Evie's dad mad.

'You've done something remarkably helpful towards possibly saving the Eco Gardens,' he says. 'You clever girl!'

I grin nervously. 'Oh . . . er . . . good! But . . . but . . . what have I done?'

'Yes, Dad, what *has* Lola done?' Evie asks. She sounds

very slightly offended, as she does not seem to be included in my amazing-but-somewhat-baffling achievement.

'Let me explain,' says her dad. 'If a rare or endangered species is discovered living and, even more importantly, breeding on a site, then that site can be declared an SSSI – or Site of Special Scientific Interest. In other words, the land is protected. But of course it doesn't automatically mean that the Eco Gardens can afford to keep going. The council could still refuse to renew the lease. So your petition and Fun Day are still important.'

'It's all beginning to sound more hopeful,' Evie's mum comments. 'As long as the Golden Orioles stay in the woodland and don't decide to move into my house.' She has obviously not completely recovered from her bird phobia and the Pablo incident.

'It's really cool,' says Evie. 'Well done, Lola!' She turns to her dad. 'Dad, please can I have a camera phone like Lola's? Now that you know how really useful they are!'

Everyone laughs, although I think that Evie is serious.

Wanda is busily scribbling in her reporter's notepad, and her tape recorder is switched on, as usual.

'We should call Kate and tell her the news,' I say.

'Go ahead,' says Evie's dad.

When we have phoned Kate, who is thrilled at the news and says that she should have realised immediately that the land would be protected but her mind was on other things, we quickly check Your Say on the council website, and are amazed to see that the Whisperer/Amelia has not given up.

```
Whisperer: It's a conspiracy! They're
trying to cover up the massive danger
we are all in because of all the germs
at the Eco Gardens. There are great
piles of POO everywhere! No wonder
the place is a public health hazard –
it should be closed down so that some-
thing better can be built there.
```

'Pathetic!' Evie exclaims.

'She doesn't give up,' I comment.

Outside, the clouds are piling up, looming dark grey overhead and presently blotting out the sun. Just as it goes dark and the first low rumble of thunder is heard in the distance, we hear the jingle of Meltonio's ice-cream van as it turns into Frog Street. The van's battery must be low as the jingle is very slow.

Evie turns off the computer, and we run downstairs and, because the storm is still away in the distance, out into the street to tell Meltonio our news. Meltonio is delighted to hear about the Golden Orioles. He says he hopes that Plunkett's evil plot can now be stopped, and launches into an angry speech about how much he has disliked David Plunkett ever since he fired him from a job he had working in the cafeteria at Plunkett's Plastics

Retail Heaven, the large superstore in the nearby town of Rippingham, which we are planning to visit with Liam.

Meltonio tells us that his dismissal came at a time when Mrs Meltonio was about to give birth to their seventh child, Domenico. 'Mr Plunkett is a nasty man,' says Meltonio, with distaste. 'So now I sell ice-cream – a much better job.'

MELTONIO

The thunder is rolling nearer and it is starting to make me nervous. Meltonio says that we had better go indoors. We quickly buy two Totally Tutti Frutti Ices before waving goodbye as Meltonio very slowly heads for home to charge his van's battery – and the jingle.

It has been steadily getting darker all the while we have been outside talking to Meltonio and I have been getting increasingly agitated. Suddenly there is a flash which lights up Frog Street and, seconds later, a loud crack of thunder nearly overhead sends us scurrying to my house – I nearly drop my ice-cream!

'Mad!' exclaims Evie, breathlessly, as we get inside and close the door. 'Eating ice-cream in a storm! Are you OK, Lola?' She knows that I don't like storms.

I nod my head and start giggling with relief at being indoors. It has been an amazing day and I feel so proud and happy that Evie and I have both been able to help to save the Eco Gardens. No amount of storm and rain can possibly dampen my high spirits. All is well! Can anything cloud a perfect day?

There is a light on in the kitchen, and I hear Mum's voice, 'Is that you, Lola? I'm glad you're back – it's not very nice outside, is it? Come and join me, and tell me what you've been up to.'

'Certainly, Mum! Evie and I have got loads to —'

A clap of thunder drowns out what I say next, which is probably just as well because, as I step into the kitchen, I am confronted by a mum with bright red hair. It is not the same rich, autumnal shade of red as Evie's hair – this is full-on carrot. I had only just got used to mum being a blonde.

'Mum . . .!'

Dad is sitting at the kitchen table with his laptop, and a lot of papers and receipts. He and mum have been doing their accounts. Also on the table – and there is a clap of thunder and my stomach turns over as I see it – is a Plunkett's Plastics catalogue.

'Do you like it?' Mum asks.

'No, it's horrible!' I exclaim, staring at the loathsome catalogue. 'I hate it! It's awful! Throw it away!'

Mum looks shocked. 'Er, I didn't think it was *that* bad,' she falters, nervously touching her hair. 'And I can't throw my hair away . . .'

'Oh! Er, no – I didn't mean your hair, Mum! Your hair looks . . . great! I meant THAT catalogue.'

'Don't throw it away,' says Evie. 'Put it in the recycling bin.'

Mum looks confused. 'Why?' she asks. 'There's some quite useful stuff in there. Dad and I were thinking of going to the Rippington store tomorrow to have a look around.' She picks up the catalogue. 'Look at this, darling.' She shows me a page full of pictures of tacky pink plastic bedroom furniture. 'I thought that some of those storage boxes would be useful for you, and the pink inflatable bedside table is fun, isn't it?'

'Mum! I am *sooo* too old for stuff like that!' I explode. 'Why didn't you just have me christened Barbie and have done with it? And why can't we have a green car like Evie's parents have just got, instead of our old white van?'

'Green car?' says Dad, sounding confused. 'Why green? Why not white, or any other colour?'

Evie, who has always been good at defusing potentially-explosive situations – usually involving me and my mum – steps in and hastily explains the whole Plunkett situation, and our adventures today.

Mum and Dad are open-mouthed with amazement. Mum recovers first and gives me a big hug – my ice-cream nearly gets squished! Then she hugs Evie and gets some of Evie's ice-cream in her hair. Dad says he thinks he'll open a bottle of home-made ginger beer, which explodes all over the kitchen. I apologise to Evie for my parents being completely mad. She says that she's used to mad parents – we both are. Dad calms down, and offers to lend a marquee for the Fun Day.

'That would be great, Dad. Liam's band could play in there, especially if it rains, and there could be refreshments, and stuff.'

Mum is gazing wistfully at the Plunkett's catalogue. 'I'd still like to go there,' she says. 'That plastic filing cabinet would be useful.'

'But Mum!' I protest. 'It's not biodegradable! It's plastic rubbish, destined for landfill! And do you really still want to go there after all we've told you about Plunkett's evil plot?'

Evie nudges me and whispers, 'Perhaps we could have a lift, if your parents are going there tomorrow?'

Realising that Evie's suggestion makes sense, as we had planned to go to Plunkett's Plastics Retail Heaven one day with Liam, I swallow my anger and ask Dad if we can come along, and bring Liam too, if they are going tomorrow.

Dad looks surprised, but says yes. 'I just hope the van will start,' he adds. 'Bob at the garage said he's fixed it, and it should be OK for another few months.'

Outside, the storm has died away, and a shaft of sunlight breaks through the clouds. I remember that this is a *good* day, and nothing should be allowed to spoil it.

More Dodo facts:
1) She loves dolphins – so do Evie and I.
2) She loves ice-cream – so do Evie and I.
3) She plays electric guitar as well as singing – this is *sooo* cool!

4) She loves travelling and meeting people.
5) Her greatest wishes are for world peace and an end to global warming. She is *definitely* our favourite singer.

Eco-fact Number Nine:

Only the Adelie and the Emperor penguins can survive life on the Antartic mainland. The Adelie penguin lays two eggs in a nest made of stones, in December, the warmest month in Antartica.

Chapter Ten

'Cool!'

To my surprise, Liam seems pleased at the opportunity to have a ride in our clapped-out white van.

'It would be great for the band,' Liam enthuses. 'We could transport all our stuff to gigs.'

'As long as it didn't break down on the way,' I remark.

Dad laughs as we turn into the huge car park which surrounds Plunkett's Plastics Retail Heaven. 'At least she got us here today,' he says – he often refers to the van as if it is female, except when it breaks down, then he refers to it in the sort of language I am not meant to repeat.

Plunkett's Plastics Retail Heaven – or Hell on Earth, as I prefer to think of it – is huge, with wide aisles full of shelf upon shelf packed with plastic rubbish for every room in your house AND for your garden. There are even plastic kennels for dogs and a plastic fountain and fish pond, complete with plastic fish, watched closely by a plastic heron. 'I suppose you could have real fish if you wanted to,' observes Evie. 'But the people who come here probably prefer plastic ones.'

Mum insists on stopping at the cafeteria for a drink. The tables, the chairs, the knives, forks and spoons are all made of Plunkett's plastic – even the food looks as though it is made of plastic, and, according to Dad who has a cheese sandwich, it tastes like plastic too.

While Mum goes to look at plastic filing cabinets – despite grim warnings from me about global meltdown – Evie and I wander up and down the aisles, expressing eco-worrier outrage at the tons of plastic. Liam seems to find our outrage funny, and pursues us along one of the aisles clutching two horrible plastic gnomes.

'These gnomes are sorry they've upset you!' he says, adding in a high-pitched voice, 'We're so sorry! We're so sorry! We're friendly little gnomes – we really are! Please take us home!'

'No!' says Evie.

'Sh!' I hiss suddenly. 'Be quiet! Look over there!'

Standing nearby, with their backs to us, are two youths, stacking shelves. They are wearing purple Plunkett's Plastics staff T-shirts and are talking in clearly audible voices.

'I still can't believe we got away with it,' says one of the youths, who has a shaven head and an earring. It is Dean!

'You *think* we got away with it,' says the other youth, who is taller, his dark hair tied back in a short ponytail. 'But you had to go and drop those wire cutters – *and* you were an idiot to use them without gloves on: they'll have your fingerprints all over them.'

'It wasn't my fault! You went and left the gloves behind, remember? You were meant to bring them. And then those stupid monkeys started screaming.'

'Stupid creatures! Almost as stupid as that parrot! I even got it to say "Stupid parrot"! I kept going back to see it and repeating "Stupid parrot". Eventually it said it back to me!'

'Has Plunkett paid you yet?'

'No, he said we didn't do the job properly. It's the same as when we dropped the penguin – he didn't pay us then either, even though I did what he asked and phoned the radio station about the kidnapping. But he said I messed up because I dumped the penguin in a garden instead of somewhere more public. But it was struggling inside my jacket and then it pooed on my shirt!' Dean sounds disgusted. He continues, 'And Plunkett had the cheek to send a letter to the papers with *my* name on it – even though he changed it a bit. I know he sent other letters with fake names, too.'

'I'm not doing no more jobs for him.'

'Me neither.'

Dean looks round, and Evie and I quickly turn and walk away, slowly at first, and then, as soon as we have turned the corner and are out of sight of the two youths, we race to find Mum and Dad. I am worried in case Dean and the other youth are coming after us. Liam follows at a more laid-back pace.

'Oh, where are Mum and Dad?' I gasp. 'This place is too big.'

We eventually find them in the furthest aisle, pushing a trolley with a big purple plastic filing cabinet in it.

'Hello,' says Dad. 'Seen anything interesting?'

Evie and I exchange glances. 'We certainly have,' I reply.

'We've found the people who stole Pablo!' Evie says in a low voice. 'So we'll be able to tell the police where to find them.'

'Goodness!' exclaims Mum. 'You two don't seem to be able to go anywhere without getting involved in some kind of drama or murder-mystery!'

'No one's been murdered, Mum.'

'I suppose we'd better keep our voices down,' says Dad, cottoning on more quickly than Mum. 'We don't want to arouse suspicion until you've had a chance to talk to the police. We don't want the two youths to get alarmed and run away.'

Our chance to talk to the police comes on Thursday, when I receive an excited phone call from Evie to say that a police car has just pulled up outside her house and I had better come round immediately.

As I hurry to Evie's house, I can see Mrs Fossett's curtains twitching madly. She probably thinks that we are all about to be arrested and taken away for questioning for unmentionable crimes.

The two policemen are very grateful for all the information which Liam, Evie and I are able to give them, especially that they can find Dean Hughes at Plunkett's Plastics Retail Heaven.

'We've got some fingerprints from the wire cutters which were dropped at the scene of the crime,' says one of the officers. 'So it's just a matter of matching them – and we've got him!'

'And you'll charge him with kidnapping Pablo, won't you?' I ask.

The policemen laugh. 'Don't worry – he'll confess,' one of them replies. 'Once he realises we've got evidence against him for causing criminal damage AND we've got CCTV footage of him with the parrot, my guess is he'll panic and come clean about all of it.'

'Will you arrest David Plunkett?' Evie asks.

Her dad clears his throat nervously. 'Perhaps you should stop asking questions, dear,' he says. 'I think the officers came to ask *you* questions.'

The policemen smile.

'We'll be pursuing our inquiries,' says one of them as they get up to leave. 'Thank you very much for your help.'

'Wow!' exclaims Liam after they have left. 'A cosy chat with the cops! How do we follow *that*?'

'We could all go and bounce on the trampoline?' Evie suggests.

'Madness!' exclaims Liam. 'Let's go!'

I find it impossible to bounce properly because I am giggling so much, and we soon collapse in a hilarious heap in the middle of the trampoline. I don't think I have ever had so much fun – at least, not since the last Eco-Worriers' Pillowfight . . .!

Eco-fact Number Ninety-four:
The Golden Toad and the Harlequin Frog of Costa Rica have disappeared as a direct result of global warming.

Chapter Eleven

'I *think we'll* have it framed,' says Evie's mum.

It is the following morning, and Evie's mum and dad and Evie and I are sitting at the breakfast table with today's edition of *The Shrubberylands Sentinel* spread out in front of us. I stayed with Evie last night.

The front page of the *Sentinel* is devoted to a single story: *IT'S ECO-HEAVEN AT THE ECO GARDENS!* There's a photo of a smiling Kate Meadowsweet and, in smaller print, it says:

It has been officially confirmed that there is no truth in the rumours that there have been cases of bird flu at the Ecological Gardens, and we apologise unreservedly for any misleading impressions which this newspaper may have given in the past. Indeed, it is the most wonderful place, caring for many fascinating and endangered species, and it is open to the public every day of the year, excluding Christmas Day. There have even been confirmed sightings of the rare Golden Oriole, which is nesting in the carefully-managed woodland area. This means that the site will now be designated an SSSI (Site of Special Scientific Interest), and afforded full protection. It is good to know that our precious wildlife has a safe haven.

GOLDEN ORIOLE

Evie's mum turns the page.

'It's us!' I exclaim. I have already seen the photo of Evie and me, beside a photo of Pablo, but I get the same rush of excitement every time I see it, even if I *have* got my eyes closed in the photo, and Evie's hair is blowing across her eyes so that all you can see is her nose and her mouth grinning cheesily.

'I'm so proud!' says Evie's mum, wiping away a tear.

Underneath the photos is an article which reads:

These are the two brave girls who rescued the little penguin, Pablo (pictured), so cruelly abandoned by two youths who stole him from Penguin Paradise at the Ecological Gardens. The prompt action by the two girls — Evie Evans and Lola Woodhouse — meant that Pablo was soon reunited with his penguin pals.

If you want to see Pablo for yourself, and all the other amazing wildlife at the Ecological Gardens, why not come along this Saturday and claim a free drink in the Eco-Café with the flyer you should find in today's issue of the Sentinel *(ask your newsagent if it is missing). And DON'T MISS the Family Fun Day and concert on Saturday 12th August in aid of the Pablo Appeal to raise money and awareness about the effects of global warming. Gates open at ten in the morning. Free Pablo fun pack for every child aged ten and under!*

'We're too old!' exclaims Evie. 'Unfair!'

'Wanda's done wonders,' I say. 'She should definitely be promoted to top reporter — she's wasted on the sports pages.'

Before he leaves for work, Evie's dad comes with us to Mr Patel's shop to collect the petition so that he can take it with him to the council meeting this afternoon. We are amazed to see how many people have signed it. There are at least a hundred signatures, plus the extra ones which Evie and I have collected on separate sheets of paper.

'That's good, isn't it, Dad?' says Evie, her eyes shining.

'It certainly is, love,' says her dad, giving her a kiss before getting into his Monda Civic Hybrid with the petition, and leaving for work.

'Evie!' I exclaim suddenly. 'I can hear Meltonio's van!'

Meltonio's van comes trundling along the road and stops beside us. 'I'm going to the Eco Gardens today,' he tells us. 'Do you want to come?'

'Oh, yes!' We quickly run back to Evie's house to tell her mum, and then we join Meltonio in his van. He is gazing at the front page of the *Sentinel*, an expression of intense happiness on his face. He tells us how proud he is of us. 'You have saved one of the best places on this earth – the beautiful Eco Gardens.' And then he bursts into tears, which is rather embarrassing. Evie offers him a recycled tissue from the mini-pack in her pocket. When he has recovered, we set off, singing along to the jingle, which is playing at almost the right speed.

When we reach the car park at the Eco Gardens, we see a large crowd of people near the woodland area. Nearly all of them are peering through binoculars and carrying photographic equipment.

'Twitchers,' says Kate, coming to greet us. 'They're keen bird-watchers, and they've flocked here after reading in the paper this morning about the Golden Oriole. We've had to put up a temporary barrier to hold them back so that they don't frighten the birds away. But fortunately they're all being very reasonable, and quite a few of them have decided to look round the gardens while they're here, so it's good for business.'

The weather is warming up, and a number of twitchers come over to the van to buy ice-cream – so it is good for Meltonio's business, too. Kate thanks Evie and me profusely for *everything*, and we go with her to see Mr Macawber.

Kate says that he is so much better – in fact he is back to his old self – that she is planning to take him to the Shrubberylands Shopping Zone this afternoon for a short wander through the crowds to help publicise the Fun Day. Two other keepers are bringing Monty the Royal Python and Dave the Chameleon. Kate asks us if we would like to come along and we say that we would love to.

Shrubberylands Shopping Zone is heaving with summer-holiday shoppers, and Evie and I follow Kate, who has Mr Macawber perched on her shoulder, and the other two keepers, who are carrying Monty the Royal Python and Dave the Chameleon, through the crowds. Most people are fascinated. Kate asks them politely to look but not to touch, so that the animals don't become too stressed, and tells them about the Fun Day. Several people even identify Evie and me from our photo in the paper and offer us congratulations. It is slightly embarrassing – but a nice feeling!

Then Evie tugs at my arm. 'Look!' she says. 'Over there! I don't believe it – she's copying us!'

Standing outside the Easybuy Bargainstore are Amelia and Jemima, also handing out flyers. Evie stoops to pick up one of Amelia's flyers, which has been dropped and trampled underfoot. It reads:

WHO NEEDS PENGUINS? COME TO
PLUNKETT'S PLASTICS RETAIL HEAVEN
IN RIPPINGTON ON SATURDAY 12th AUGUST
AND PICK UP SOME REAL BARGAINS –
AND GET A FREE BALLOON!

'She must have seen us handing out flyers the other day and copied our idea,' hisses Evie to me. 'And now she's trying to compete with the Family Fun Day – she must have read about it in the paper this morning – and I expect she's got a really high-powered, expensive computer which can print these out. And they're not printed on recycled paper . . .'

Evie walks over to Amelia with the Plunkett's Plastics flyer, screws it up and drops it at her feet.

'Nice try, Amelia. But you won't succeed!'

'Want to bet?'

'Yes, I don't mind. But you're not looking too good . . .'

Amelia looks worried. 'What do you mean?' she snaps.

'You're looking a bit off-colour – are you sure you haven't got penguin flu?'

'Ha ha. Very funny,' says Amelia, rolling her eyes at us. Jemima giggles until Amelia gives her a look – and she shuts up.

'Why don't you go home and take some parrotcetamol?' says Evie over her shoulder, as we start walking away.

'Get lost!' says Amelia. 'Everyone's going to come to my dad's shop. No one's interested in your stupid penguins!'

'Rubbish!' I exclaim. 'The only thing you're interested in, apart from yourself, is money. You only want people to come to your dad's shop so that he makes loads of money to spend on *you*. That's why you wanted him to have a whole business park – even *more* money. And you couldn't care less if the whole world fills up with plastic rubbish!'

Passing shoppers come between us and Amelia and Jemima, which is a relief – I want to get away from Amelia. Evie has always been more confrontational than I am, so I surprised myself just now with my long speech.

Kate says that Mr Macawber has had enough of the crowds and she had better get back to the Eco Gardens – will we be OK? Evie says that we will be fine as her mum is nearby working in her shop. We say goodbye to Kate and wander away to Evie's mum's shop.

Walking past a bench in the middle of the pedestrian precinct, we see Liam and a group of Sixth-Form friends who are in his band. We say hello, and Liam calls us over.

'So, are you up for playing a gig at the Fun Day on August the twelfth?' Evie asks Liam's friends.

She is much braver than I am about talking to Sixth Formers – I suppose it helps to have an older brother. I am standing slightly behind Evie, trying to look cool and casual.

'We've been talking about it,' Liam replies. 'We're looking forward to it. In fact, we're going to Ben's house now to practise in his garage. See you later.'

As we go into Evie's mum's shop, I notice from a distance that a lot of people are refusing to take Amelia's flyers, and she is looking *very* sulky.

We arrive home to the BEST news EVER! Evie's dad has phoned from the council meeting which he is attending, because he wanted us to know immediately that the council has looked at our petition and decided that they WILL renew Kate's lease!

'It's all working out,' says Evie happily, sticking a little cluster of green stars on her eco-chart. We are relaxing in her room at the end of the day. Earlier, Mrs Fossett, Mrs Baggot and Mrs Throgmorton came over to congratulate us and to say that they're intending to come to the Fun Day.

'*That* was seriously weird!' says Evie.

'It freaked me out a bit, too,' I agree. 'But it was nice.'

'When I saw them coming up the path, I was sure they were coming to complain,' Evie continues.

'It made such a nice change that they *weren't* complaining.'

'And I couldn't believe it when that news reporter from Shrubberylands FM turned up to interview us,' says Evie.

'Yes – it was really odd hearing our voices on the radio.' The radio station broadcast the same news item about the Eco Gardens as the one that appeared in this morning's *Sentinel* on their news bulletins later today. They also publicised the Fun Day, and said that they would go on mentioning it over the next few weeks.

Picking up the latest copy of *Green Teen* magazine off the floor, I lie on my front on Evie's bed and leaf through it.

Evie sits beside me on the bed with her list of Things to Worry About.

'There,' she exclaims. 'I've just crossed everything off it. There's nothing left to worry about!'

I turn a page of *Green Teen* magazine and something catches my eye. 'Listen to this,' I say.

Eco-fact Number Forty-five:

If everyone in the world consumed resources at the rate we do in the United Kingdom, we would need three planets to support us.

'Oh great,' says Evie. 'You've just given me something to worry about.'

Chapter Twelve

'FAMILY FUN DAY!' I shout out of Evie's bedroom window to anyone in Frog Street who has managed to remain unaware of the approaching event. Meltonio has been handing out flyers from his ice-cream van to all his customers over the last few days, and Evie and I have been telling everyone we know about it. Kate is expecting large numbers of people to turn up if it is anything like the last couple of weeks, when there has been a big response to the offer to visitors to claim free drinks in the Eco-Café. The staff were rushed off their feet serving cup after cup of Fair Trade tea, Guatemalan coffee and a range of organic fruit juices. And now – AT LAST! – the day itself has arrived.

One of the first things to do was to wake up Liam, and Evie called me early this morning to come and help her as she was having difficulty prising her brother out of bed. But by the time I arrived he was already up and in the bathroom, brushing his teeth.

'He's got the message about not leaving the tap running,' says Evie, sticking a green star on her eco-chart. 'A green star for Liam – that's a first!'

'You seem to be getting the message through to your family,' I observe. 'I'm not sure about mine. They're still enthusing about that awful plastic filing cabinet. I despair!'

'At least they're helping with the Fun Day,' Evie points out.

Mum and Dad were at the Eco Gardens yesterday putting up the marquee and some smaller tents for the various stalls and displays. This morning they are using their white van to transport Liam's band and all their instruments and speakers.

The sun is shining and there is a light breeze blowing – it is a perfect summer's day, and the swifts are wheeling and darting high in the sky.

I am observing Posh and Pout through my binoculars. 'Wow! Huge monster goldfish,' I exclaim. 'Scary!'

We are in high spirits as we go along the road in the Monda Civic to the Eco Gardens. When we get there, Evie's mum gives Evie some money so that we can go and enjoy the various stalls and attractions.

It is good to see the place already packed with people, even though the gates have only recently opened. The refreshment kiosk is doing a roaring trade, and so is Meltonio, selling his ices. He waves to us, and we wave back. Kate comes to welcome us, and thanks Evie and me and our families for all our help. Her eyes are shining as she tells us that due to a steady rise in the number of visitors recently, she will now definitely be able to keep going. Evie and I are thrilled, and Kate gives us a big hug.

There is plenty going on. As well as a bouncy castle, tombola and lucky dip, there is face-painting – you can have your face painted as the animal or bird of your choice. Shrubberylands FM is there, handing out free balloons and letting members of the public choose their favourite tunes to be played on air. The keepers are walking around with Monty the Royal Python, Colin the Corn Snake and Dave the Chameleon, for people to look at. Kate herself has Mr Macawber, and she is letting people have their photos taken with him. Evie's mum takes one look at Mr Macawber and mutters something about needing to attend to the Fashion Passion stall, which her assistant, Gabby, has set up for the day.

'Clever parrot!' I hear Mr Macawber say.

Kate tells us that she has a big surprise for us. 'Be at the big marquee just after The Rock Hyraxes have finished, and you'll find out,' she says, ignoring our pleas to tell us NOW.

I see Wanda in the distance, with the photographer from the *Sentinel*, and Evie and I rush up to her to thank her again for the wonderful article – Evie's mum already arranged for her to be sent a big bunch of flowers to show our gratitude.

Wanda says that she was just reporting the truth, and she was only too happy to do so. She tells us that she has been promoted, and is now one of the *Sentinel*'s chief news reporters.

'So was it you who reported that David Plunkett has been charged with using bribes and threats to promote his business interests, and is facing a massive fine and possibly a prison sentence pending an inquiry?' Evie asks, fishing the article out of the pocket of her blue cropped trousers. She tore it out of the paper yesterday, as she has been avidly collecting all the publicity connected with both Plunkett and the Eco Gardens for a scrapbook she's making.

'Yes, that was me,' says Wanda, smiling.

Evie and I wander along the row of little craft and food stalls. The foods on offer range from yummy to yucky. I love the organic chocolate stall, but I am not so sure about the bean and falafelburgers . . . There is a craft stall selling eco-friendly jute bags and plant-holders, and another one selling animal ornaments woven from shredded palm leaves from sustainable crops. We wave to Gabby who is selling organic T-shirts and Ethletic trainers at the Fashion Passion stall.

I notice Dad, who has been handing out cards for his tent and marquee business, is now deep in conversation with a man at the Alternative Vehicles Technology stall. We pass a group of small children who are sitting on the grass, colouring in pictures of Pablo from their special Pablo fun packs. Pablo is a celebrity now, thanks to the Pablo Appeal. His picture is everywhere – on posters, in the paper, on all the publicity material – as well as in the fun packs, and people like to spot him among the other penguins because of the distinctive white marking on his head, as well as his green tag. They also enjoy identifying the other penguins by their coloured wing tags.

'Testing . . . testing . . .' We hear someone tapping a crackly microphone, and then Kate announces over the tannoy that people are invited to go to the big marquee to see a live performance by the exciting new local band, The Rock Hyraxes. Go, Liam!

The Rock Hyraxes are a big success. When the performance ends, everyone can hear the Howler Monkeys screaming and the gibbons going *'WOOH! WOOH!'* – they obviously like The Rock Hyraxes! Everyone laughs and claps and cheers, and Liam is so thrilled with the audience reaction that he beckons Evie and me on stage and gives us a big hug. I can't stop smiling – Liam

HUGGED me! I will keep the top I'm wearing forever unwashed, since *he* touched it . . .

Kate comes on stage and thanks The Rock Hyraxes – and the Howler Monkeys and the gibbons. And then she thanks everyone for coming and supporting the Eco Gardens and the Pablo Appeal. She pays tribute to her keepers and to Evie and me for rescuing Pablo and for all our help. She goes on to mention that they now have dormice as well as Golden Orioles in the woodland. More applause.

'And now I have a special announcement,' she says, turning to Evie and me. 'And I need to thank these two wonderful girls again because it was their idea.'

Evie and I look at each other wonderingly.

'They were telling me,' Kate continues, 'about their favourite singer, Dodo – and they suggested that I invited her to come to the Eco Gardens to do a concert. I thought that she would be too busy, but then I thought that there was no harm in asking . . .'

Evie and I are now quivering with excitement.

'I didn't say anything about this to anyone,' Kate says, 'because I didn't want to cause disappointment. But this morning I received an email from Dodo herself, saying that she is willing to give a free concert here at the end of August in aid of the Eco Gardens and the Pablo Appeal, because she is passionately concerned about global warm-ing and the plight of penguins and animals everywhere.'

Evie screams. Fortunately everyone else is cheering and clapping, too, so her scream doesn't deafen too many people. We hug each other, and we hug Kate.

Then everyone cheers even more loudly, and the photographer from the *Sentinel* snaps away, as a man steps forward to present Kate with a cheque for a large sum of money donated by a local business association who have decided to support the Eco Gardens – so not all businessmen are bad!

'Can today get any better?' I say to Evie.

We decide to go to see Pablo.

'Hello, Pablo,' I say. 'This is your special day. Evie and I are going to do everything we can to make sure that you have a safe and happy home, and that your relatives in the Antarctic get to keep their home, too.'

I am not sure if he hears me, but I mean every word. Annie the Penguin Keeper, who is standing nearby, smiles at me. I smile back.

I see Dad nearby, and go to talk to him. I ask him what he was talking about to the man at the Alternative Vehicles Technology stall. Dad tells me that he's decided to have his white van converted so that it runs on lithium ion batteries, just like Meltonio's van – but without the jingle, presumably.

Dad is beaming. 'It will travel between sixty and a hundred miles on a single charge, and, with any luck, it won't break down so often, so I shouldn't have to fork out so much for repairs, and I obviously won't have to pay for petrol.'

'That's so cool, Dad!' I exclaim, giving him a hug.

Wow! My parents are going green! I must tell Evie.

'I think that was the FUNNEST Family Fun Day EVER!' exclaims Evie, as we relax in her room later.

'I've never seen so many people having a good time,' I comment. 'It was great to see them enjoying themselves and admiring the animals.'

'And everyone loved it when Meltonio sang.'

'Yes, I think he could be an opera singer.'

I am lying on my back on Evie's bed, looking at the penguin poster and the wallchart on her ceiling. I feel happier and healthier from my organic diet and my training for the Olympics.

'*Is* there anything left to worry about?' I ask.

'Your mum's hair?'

'Apart from that.'

'The world coming to an end?'

'That's quite worrying.'

'No it isn't.'

'Why isn't it?'

'Because we won't LET it come to an end. Eco-worriers will triumph!'

'Evie?'

'Yes?'

'Will you always be my friend?'

'Yes, of course! You don't need to worry about THAT!'

'No, you're right. That's the one thing I don't need to worry about.'

'And will you always be *my* friend?' Evie asks.

'Of course!'

'In that case,' says Evie firmly, 'there really is NOTHING to worry about.'

'Apart from composting toilets,' I say.

'What?'

'At one of the stands today – the Waste Management one – they were showing this composting toilet where you collect and recycle all your own —'

'OK! OK! Enough! That really IS a worrying thought.'

'I know. But we are ECO-WORRIERS!'

Honeysuckle Lovelace

Cherry Whytock

The Dog Walkers' Club

There comes a time in almost everybody's life when they have a brilliant idea. Honeysuckle Lovelace's Brilliant Idea is to set up a Dog Walkers' Club with her friends. But they become suspicious of one of their clients and the Dog Walkers' Club provides perfect cover for investigation!

Ghosthunters

A new client brings a new investigation for Honeysuckle and her friends. When they dog-sit Twitters, the twitchy whippet, they become convinced that the house is haunted and that it's time to find the ghost and set it free.

Girl Writer

Ros Asquith

Features top writing tips for aspiring authors!

Castles and Catastrophes

Cordelia Arbuthnott wants to write books. Not the sort that her aunt, the bestselling children's author Laura Hunt writes, but literary masterpieces. A writing competition at her dreaded new school seems just the opportunity, but writing a masterpiece is trickier than she expected; real life just keeps getting in the way.

Sleuths and Truths

Cordelia loves to read about Sherlock Holmes and now writes about his younger sister, Shirley Holmes and her stories. But Cordelia discovers a real life mystery to solve as she is convinced a man has been wrongly convicted. But is she right?

SeaGirls

g.g. elliot

The Crystal City

Finding out that she can breathe underwater is only the beginning of Polly's discoveries.

Even before this, she's always felt different. But then she finds a kindred spirit in Lisa. The two girls discover that they both have the same fish-shaped birthmark, were both adopted, and can both breathe underwater. Surely it can't just be coincidence?

When a strong current drags them to the depths of the ocean, they not only discover their true identities, but an amazing world – more incredible and more disturbing than they could ever have imagined . . .

Venus Spring

JONNY ZUCKER

Stunt★Girl

Venus Spring is fourteen and this is the first summer she's been allowed to go to stunt camp. It is a dream come true – something she has been working towards for years. But while she is there, she stumbles on a devious and terrifying plot that threatens the surrounding countryside, and Venus is determined to uncover it.

Body★Double

When DCI Radcliff hears a rumour that a gang intends to kidnap teen movie star Tatiana Fairfleet, she asks Venus to act as Tatiana's body double at her boarding school – providing a decoy if there are any problems. But Venus soon finds herself in real danger, and needs to rely on all her stunt skills to stop events spiralling out of control.

www.piccadillypress.co.uk

☆ The latest news on forthcoming books

☆ Chapter previews

☆ Author biographies

☆ Fun quizzes

☆ Reader reviews

☆ Competitions and fab prizes

☆ Book features and cool downloads

☆ And much, much more . . .

Log on and check it out!

Piccadilly Press